JENNY McLACHLAN

FLIRTY DANCING

FEIWEL AND FRIENDS
NEW YORK

A FEIWEL AND FRIENDS BOOK
An Imprint of Macmillan

Feiwel and Friends books may be purchased for business or promotional use. For
information on bulk purchases, please contact the Macmillan Corporate and Premium
Sales Department at (800) 221-7945 x5442 or by e-mail at specialmarkets@macmillan.com.

Library of Congress Cataloging-in-Publication Data

McLachlan, Jenny.
Flirty dancing / Jenny McLachlan. — First U.S. edition.
pages cm
"First published in Great Britain by Bloomsbury Publishing Plc."
Summary: "Shy Bea finds herself paired with Ollie—the cutest guy in school—for a dance
competition. Bea's life is transformed as she finally gets her time in the spotlight"—
Provided by publisher.
ISBN 978-1-250-06148-5 (hardback) — ISBN 978-1-250-08013-4 (ebook)
[1. Interpersonal relations—Fiction.   2. Dance—Fiction.   3. Contests—Fiction.
4. Bashfulness—Fiction.   5. Schools—Fiction.]   I. Title.
PZ7.1.M4357Fli 2015   [Fic]—dc23   2014042422

First published in the United States by Feiwel and Friends, an imprint of Macmillan

Book design by April Ward

Feiwel and Friends logo designed by Filomena Tuosto

First U.S. Edition: 2015

1   3   5   7   9   10   8   6   4   2

macteenbooks.com

LiTTLE LADYBiRDS NURSERY

"I'm afraid I do not find this funny," says Miss Cherry, frowning at the four girls sitting cross-legged in front of her. "As I've told you before, I do not like you playing rude pirates. Don't laugh, Pearl. Showing your underwear is not the behavior of a pirate, and it is certainly *not* the behavior of a Ladybird. Kat, Betty, *please* sit still. Now, while I hand round the milk, I want you all to think very carefully about how *nice* pirates would behave. Bea, don't eat that: It's for the rabbit."

1.

TEN YEARS,
FOUR STARTER-BRAS &
ONE BIG FIGHT LATER...

A small naked person is licking me. I don't panic—this happens a lot. The naked person starts kissing my face. I smell peanut butter and banana and . . . hang on . . . the person is not entirely naked. It's wearing wellies. *Wellies?* This is new. And *totally* unacceptable.

I grope for my phone . . . 5:34 a.m.

5:34 *a.m.*!

"Bea!" Emma cries. "Happy birthday!"

"Go away. It is *not* my birthday." I try to push her out of my bed, but she resists and we start to scuffle. Mistake. For a three-year-old, my sister's a mean wrestler. I briefly consider being grown-up, but before I know it we're having a real fight.

"I got you a present!" comes her muffled voice from somewhere around my feet.

"Present later?" I could probably sleep with her down there. It's not so bad, quite cozy and—

"PRESENT NOW!" she screams.

She's clearly in one of her extra-special moods so I say what I always say when I want to get rid of her. "Did you hear that, Emma?"

"What?"

"I heard Dad's voice . . . He's home! Dad's home!" (He isn't. He's in Mexico.)

"Daddy!" She shoots out of my bed and down the stairs, leaving me to roll over and snuggle my face into something warm and mushy. A forgotten bit of banana, perhaps?

I sniff it. It's not banana.

After taming my wild hair with straighteners, I do a quick zit check and put on my uniform. Then I eat toast and watch cartoons with Emma. I have to keep one hand free to stop her from drawing on my face. Personally, I don't believe a fairy on my cheek will make me "look pretty."

She comes to the door to see me off to school. Head-butting me in the stomach, she shouts, "Love you, frog-nose!" Birds fly off our neighbor's roof.

"Love you, botty-breath," I say, pushing her firmly back into the house before walking down the path. Now is the time *the shyness* sweeps over me and I leave Real Bea at home and take Shy Bea to school.

Already, as I walk to the bus stop, Shy Bea is making me hunch my shoulders and stare at the floor. The farther I get from my house, with Emma's broken slide lying on the patch of shabby lawn and our red front door, the less I feel like me.

"Though she be but little, she is fierce!" I whisper under my breath as I approach the juniors who hang out on the wall outside the store. I sit in my usual spot away from the others and get out my phone. One of the boys throws an M&M at me. It bounces off my head and lands on my lap. He laughs and watches to see what I will do. I stare at it. It's blue.

Though she be but little, she is fierce, I think.

Eat the M&M, Bea! Go on, EAT IT!

I brush it to the floor. Not my fiercest moment.

I've pretty much made myself invisible by the time the bus arrives, and when I sit next to Kat she doesn't even look up. She's staring into the tiny mirror she always carries somewhere on her person. At first, I think she's just checking out the perfectness of her blond, blond hair, but then she grabs my arm and pulls me closer, hissing, "Look behind us!"

I peer back through the bus. "What?"

"It's *him*: Ollie 'The Hug' Matthews. Oh, God. Don't look! Look! No. Don't look. OK. Look now. Soooo hot!" I sneak a sideways glance at her. Just as I suspected, her mouth is half open and her eyes are all big and puppy-like. She's doing her "Sexy Lady Face." She looks like Emma when she's doing "a big one" on the potty.

"Don't look at me," she says, "look at *him*."

And so I look. For once, I can see what she's getting at. Ollie Matthews has got these kind, brown eyes, sort of tousled hair and shoulders that look a bit like *man* shoulders and his hands are . . .

"Bean, are you listening?" Kat snaps her mirror shut. "I think I need to be more realistic and forget about juniors and focus on sophomores. Also, well, maybe he's *the one*? There was 'The Hug,' after all."

"What? He said that was an accident."

Kat snorts. "It didn't *feel* like an 'accident'!"

"He thought you were his sister. You've got the same coat . . . that one with the birds on it."

"He. Is. So. So. Hot. Don't you think?" says Kat, ignoring my little slice of REALITY.

The Hug is listening to his iPod and looking out of the window in a, you know, *hot* type of way, with his eyes, which are open (sexily), looking at trees . . . hot trees covered in sexy green leaves. "Yeah, Kat," I say. "Ollie seems—"

"Say it!" Kat is gleeful. "Go on, say it. Say Ollie Matthews is HOT." I shut my mouth. "Say it say it say it!"

"OK. I can see, from your point of view, that he could be described as . . . hot."

"Yes! He *totally* is." She grabs my arm. "Now tell me *everything* you know!"

I have a great memory. "Sophomore," I say.

"I know that."

"Was in *Bugsy Malone* last year."

"Who was he?"

"Bugsy."

"That's good, isn't it?"

"Yes."

"More," she demands hungrily.

"Rugby team."

"Mmmmm."

"Captain of the rugby team."

"MMMMM."

"Sang that song at Celebration Evening with his band."

"What song?"

"'Do Ya Think I'm Sexy?'" I sing under my breath.

"Bean. Don't."

"OK. Sorry."

"More?"

I look back at The Hug. "He rolls his sleeves up, you know, all the time, and his arms are . . ." I trail off. I refuse to use *that* word again.

Kat looks at me with slightly narrowed eyes. "I need your math book," she says. "I've forgotten to do my homework." She sits back, a smile on her face.

Kat always "forgets" to do her homework, and I always show her mine. I guess it's one of our BFF things. I scrabble around in my bag, but instead of my math book I pull out something hard, hairy and plastic.

"What is *that*?" Kat sounds disgusted.

Whoa! I'm clasping a naked Barbie doll by the head. I say naked, but her "ninny"—as Emma insists on calling that area—has been carefully colored in with blue felt-tip and embellished with glitter and, I look closer, are those *tea leaves*? "It's Ralph!" I say, laughing.

"Ralph?" Definitely no laugh.

"Emma's doll. She *said* she had a present for me and I guess this is it. Ralph's named after our neighbors' German shepherd."

"I don't care who your weirdo little sister named it after. Get rid of it!"

"Look." I show her the collaged area. Kat shrinks away. "So funny. She's supposed to look like Mum . . . not that Mum's got a glittery—" But at that moment, the bus shoots around a corner and Ralph flies out of my hand and rolls down the aisle.

"Bea, you loser, get it!"

I start rummaging around people's feet and bags.

"Bean!" comes a voice from the back of the bus. "Have you lost your Barbie?"

I look up. Oh no. This is so, so bad. *Pearl Harris* has Ralph. She's reclining on the backseat—surveying her empire—her endless, smooth brown legs draped over a boy's lap. Ralph is dangling between two blue nails that are now flecked with glitter and tea leaves.

I walk towards her. To think I once swapped underwear with this girl. (Disney ones, Ariel . . . back in the days of the Ladybirds.)

"Jelly Bean, why did you bring your *doll* to school?" The back row collapses in unison at Pearl's *amazing* sense of humor. It was Pearl who first gave me the affectionate nickname "Bean" and then, many years later, turned it into a cruel nickname by shrieking, "She's wobbling like a JELLY BEAN!" in PE. So annoying. Jelly beans don't *wobble*. They're actually quite firm.

"Hello? Is this your little girlfriend?" She gives Ralph a big kiss and then leans forward and tries to smooch the doll into my mouth. I push it away, swaying as the bus picks up speed. "Oh my God," says Pearl, looking closer at Emma's "art." "You've pimped its panties!"

I resist the temptation to try to snatch the doll back,

and next Pearl shoves Ralph's feet towards my nostrils. Her gang cackles and then stares in silence, waiting for the show to continue. I don't say or do anything. I just stand there, praying she'll get bored. "So, d'you want it back?"

"It's my sister's," I say.

There's this tiny moment where I see Pearl think, *You have a sister? Since when?* But then she snaps back with, "Yeah, right." And, "Ha-ha-ha," go her gang. "She's got *beautiful* hair," she adds, stroking the doll's thick, matted hair. "It's just like yours, Bean."

Suddenly, she leans across the seat in front of her—Ollie's seat—and holds the doll out of the window. Ollie turns around to see what's going on and slowly pulls out one of his earphones. Pearl pushes Ralph out even farther, a big smile on her stupid face.

Now I *have* to say something: Emma loves Ralph more than she loves me. "Give it back, Pearl," I say trying to grab the doll. "It's my sister's favorite!"

But she just pushes it out even farther, "Ahh. Is dis your favorwit Barbie dat you cuddle in bed?"

Slowly—he does everything slowly—Ollie reaches up, takes the doll from Pearl and throws it in my direction. Of course, I don't catch it and have to scrabble about on the floor of the bus.

When I stand up, Ollie is sharing his earphones with

Pearl. Their faces are so close together it's hard to tell where Ollie's ear ends and Pearl's lips begin. Luckily, I'm forgotten.

"That was beyond embarrassing," says Kat as I slump back in my seat, cheeks flaming. "You are an *embarrassment*, Bean."

"I know. Sorry." I shove Ralph back in my bag and we sit in silence until we get to school.

By the time we go into assembly, I'm 99 percent forgiven and Kat even links arms with me. Mrs. Pollard, our head teacher, launches straight into trash cans. The woman is trash can obsessed. "Not only is it unhygienic to put the seventh graders in them," she says, "it is also *very* mean."

She hovers over her laptop tutting and humphing and tapping until a photo of a trash can appears on the projector with a red cross over it. In the middle of the cross is a tiny face representing an Ashton Park pupil. Her mouth relaxes into a smile. "So, remember, freshmen," she says. "Trash cans are Out of Bounds. Any other announcements?"

"Just one," calls Miss Hewitt, our dance teacher, jogging to the front. "Right, freshmen, I've got some big news . . ." She pauses dramatically. "You could all be on TV!" There are murmurs of interest. "I've been sent information about a new TV talent show called *Starwars*. Think *Britain's Got Talent* for teens. There's going to be a series for singers, one for actors, one for comedians, you get the idea. Anyway, the good news is that the first one's for, wait for it . . . dancers! Yay!"

While Miss Hewitt does a celebratory moonwalk, there are a few groans, mainly from the boys, but loads more whoops, even a small one from me, and I am *not* a whooper. The girls in our year are dance crazy, and in the safety of my bedroom (door shut, curtains closed, phones handed in at the door), I *love* dancing.

"What d'you win?" comes a voice from the back.

Mrs. P draws in a breath, but Miss Hewitt gets there first. "Over the summer, the winners get professional training at stage school. Then they perform in a West End musical. Oh, and it will all be on TV, of course." Whispers ripple around the hall. "If you're going to make it to the TV stage, you need to go to an audition and Brighton's hosting one next Thursday. Anyone can audition. You can dance on your own or as a group, in any style, to any type of music. Let me know if you need more details."

Now everyone starts talking at once. "Calm down, calm down!" shouts Mrs. P, her voice rising the more she's ignored. I keep quiet, obviously.

"Hey, Bea," whispers Kat. "Let's do it! I'll ask Pearl if we can be with her. She's an *amazing* dancer!" There is so much wrong with this idea that I don't know where to start, but before I can say anything—like, "Hello? We haven't been friends since we were *seven*"—Kat leans forward and speaks to Pearl.

Pearl shakes her head, then turns to look at me. I stare straight ahead, but I can still *feel* her startling blue eyes studying me, taking everything in. I blush and Pearl smiles before turning back, her black hair remaining perfectly piled, her perfume floating across me like a spell. Mrs. P yells a decisive "QUIET!" and the hall falls silent.

Kat says under her breath, "Don't worry, Bean. I can sort it out at lunchtime. We're having our first practice in the gym!"

"Beatrice Hogg, *stand up!*" Mrs. P points a finger in my direction and two hundred pairs of eyes follow that finger. I get to my feet, my granola trampolining about in my stomach. "You will join me at lunchtime to pick up trash for the trash cans . . ." She pauses and tries to control her anger. She fails. "And you can remain standing for the rest of assembly."

No. No. NO!

And so I have to stand, head hanging, while the captain of the volleyball team gives a detailed match report including a slow-mo replay of the winning shot, followed by Mr. Higgs guiding us through the "18 Steps to Safe Internet Use."

He takes *a lot* of questions. The first is from Carl

Fisher: "Sir, if I'm online chatting with a hot girl, how do I know it's not you?"

Mr. Higgs's misguided response: "It *could* be me, Carl!"

A soccer ball flies past my head.

"Kick it back," yells a boy. I pretend not to hear him—and the insult that follows—and plod forward, picking up half a panini with the single washing-up glove Mrs. P has given me. I spot Kat coming towards me across the field. We meet at the cage: PE humiliation zone/illicit smoking area.

"Sorry about this, Bea."

"Yeah, well, I'm almost finished now." I wave my bulging bin bag around.

"No, I don't mean what happened in assembly," she says, looking into the cage rather than at me. "It's just that the other girls all think four is better than five, and Pearl doesn't think that you're that into dancing and stuff."

"What d'you mean?"

"You know . . . the dance competition. Pearl thinks it should just be her, me, Holly and Lauren."

"Not into dancing? We're *always* dancing! We've spent half our lives making up dances in our bedrooms." My eyes feel suspiciously like they might cry. I curl up my toes in my shoes. (A stop-crying trick Mum taught me—it's pretty good.)

"Also, Bea, you're sort of the wrong shape . . . a bit shorter and, well, less skinny."

"What's that got to do with it?" I say, gripping the trash bag.

"Pearl thinks the judges will be wanting a certain look," says Kat, biting her lip and fiddling with her phone. "You're all curvy and stuff and you've got all that hair. Look, Bea, can't you just—" She breaks off and sniffs. Is she about to cry? Is she pretending to cry to get out of this? "It's really hard for me, you know?" Our eyes meet and she takes this as a good sign and smiles . . . bravely. "Maybe you could enter with Betty? You used to hang out together loads."

That is the understatement of the decade. *We* used to hang out together *always*: me, Kat, Betty and Pearl. We were a gang. We were the Ladybirds! We were inseparable, but as we got older we drifted apart, and by the time we came to secondary school . . . it just wasn't the same anymore.

Kat is still my best friend, but every now and then she does something *really* mean, something that hurts. I want to rub the tuna panini in her face . . . but I also need her to be my best friend. So I just do a little smile, and say, "Don't worry about it. I didn't want to do it anyway."

"Cool, thanks, Bea," she says, her shoulders relaxing. "*I knew* you wouldn't be bothered. Pearl said you'd freak. As if. You're awesome, know?"

Pathetically, a small part of me glows at these words. "OK," I say. "I'd better take this to Mrs. P."

"Speak to you later?" She looks sort of embarrassed.

"Yeah . . . definitely." And I hobble across the field, screwing up my toes as tight as they'll go.

After school, I wait for Kat by our lockers. Soon, it feels spookily empty and teachers start giving me sympathetic looks. Time to leave.

Five minutes later I get a text: **sorry b cant get bus :'(hv dance practice!! luv Kat xxxx**. Those are guilty-sounding kisses.

When I get home, I run up to my bedroom, slam the door and throw myself down on my bed, finally admitting that I really *do* want to take part in *Starwars*. I'd never tell Kat, but the moment Miss Hewitt mentioned it I began to imagine the two of us making up a routine, nothing amazing, but something a bit different. We'd go to the auditions and, obviously, we wouldn't get through, but the other girls in our year would like it and suddenly *the shyness* would disappear and I'd be "in" with that magic freshman group where everything is so easy and fun.

But that was never going to happen.

I love dancing, but I'm not a natural, not like Kat and Pearl. I just don't look like her or the others. She's right. I *am* the wrong shape. You know skinny jeans? They won't fit me ever, ever, ever. I thought *Starwars* would change this little fact.

I roll on my side. My room usually makes me happy. The carpet's thick and dark pink and my quilt has the thinnest, softest feel. Also, I'm surrounded by flowers. Nan gives me her old gardening magazines and I cut out the flowers and stick them all over the walls. Mum was annoyed at first, but gave up when they started to creep onto the ceiling and out of the door.

My eyes drift to my bedside table where I dropped my phone. It is cluttered with pens, Playskool people (not mine), a pile of books and . . . *What* is *that*? I sit up and grab the glass of water I keep by my bed.

Something is in there. Something pink and white. Slowly, it turns round in the water to face me, or should I say *grin* at me? They are teeth. I'm staring at a big pair of grinning teeth!

"Hello, love," says a familiar voice from the doorway.

Oh.

It appears that my grandmother has moved into my bedroom. My heart sinks. How much bad news can one girl handle in a day? "Hiya, Nan," I say, quickly taking in all the nannish evidence that is scattered around: a stack of *Heat* magazines, the pillow-case-sized underwear drying on the radiator, the whiff of Chanel No. 5, and the electric blanket on my bed (I *thought* it was extra cozy). "What are you doing here . . . in your onesie?"

She *should* be watching *Countdown* in her sheltered housing on the other side of town.

"Surprise!" she lisps—it's hard to talk without teeth. She must realize this because she fishes them out of my glass of water and pops them back in. "Best not drink that, love," she says. "My apartment's flooded. Doreen upstairs put a cake in her washing machine and it just kept spinning and pumping out water all day. It was like a foam party in the communal lounge. Your mum had to come and rescue me."

She sits down at my vanity and begins rolling tiny blue rollers into her hair. Suddenly, I feel like a visitor in my own bedroom. "Now, what's up with you, grumpy face?"

"School was the worst," I say, curling up my toes so hard they hurt. Then I tell her about the whole disastrous day. While she listens, she powders her bosom with a huge powder puff and begins to file her nails. By the time Mum calls me down to tea, she's given them two coats of Lush Tangerine.

"Don't worry, Bea, love," she says. "I've got the perfect plan to teach those nasty girls a lesson."

Uh-oh . . . but just as she's about to explain, Mum shouts at me to lay the table. Nan flops down on my bed, spilling Beanie Babies onto the floor, and starts tapping away on her iPhone. "Go and help your mum," she says as I leave the room. "Nan'll sort it all out!"

First she invades my bedroom and now she's working on a plan to destroy my social life! Maybe Mum can help. In the hallway, I meet Emma, who has dry spaghetti taped to her cheeks, a grape up each nostril and a pair of Mum's tights tucked into the back of her underwear. She is mostly naked although she has colored in a lot of her body with green felt-tip.

"I'm a green cat," she informs me, then rubs herself against my legs and rolls on the floor. "Tickle!" she instructs. I tickle her tummy and just when I'm thinking how great it is to have a little cat-sister she bites my hand. I try to shake her off, but the more I shake the harder she bites.

I go into the kitchen, dragging her in behind me. Mum's rummaging about in the fridge. "There's a postcard from Dad on the table," she says, emerging with some cheese. "He got it signed!"

I pick it up. "No, he didn't."

"He got Robert Pattinson to sign it for you . . . It says 'For Bea, love, *Robert Pattinson*.' "

"Well, this has been signed by a Robert *Pattingstone*,

who, I suspect, is one of Dad's friends pretending to be Robert Pattinson because Dad forgot to do the ONE thing I asked him to do in Tijuana."

"Well, bless him for trying," she says, stopping what she's doing to bend down and stroke her cat-daughter. Dad makes props for films: giant ice-cream cones, aliens, that kind of thing. He's one of those weirdy-beardies who you see on "making of" DVDs. The old dudes who go on about how it took them eight weeks to craft one elf sword out of papier-mâché and goat hair, when all you really want to see are the bloopers. For the past three months he's been in Mexico making helmets for gnomes.

Right now, Mum's got a slightly manic look on her face so I don't make a fuss about Dad being a big fat liar, Nan (*his* mother) staying in my room or Ralph's trip to school with me. She's an ER nurse and gets pretty stressed saving lives and NEVER seeing her husband. Instead, I sit back and enjoy my fried egg with baked bean "hair," smiley ketchup face and mashed potato beard. It's supposed to be Dad.

Emma's allowed to lap up her yolk, cat-style. Gross.

"It's all sorted, love," says Nan, wandering in to our room later that evening. She waves her phone triumphantly. "You know, your *dancing* problem."

I stop blowing up my airbed. "What do you mean?"

"Well, I just had a chat with Lulu, my old dance teacher, and she's got a partner for you! She'll give you a crash course so you can be ready for the auditions on Thursday."

"A crash course? What in?"

"Jive . . . rock and roll . . . you know, like in the film *Grease*." She looks very pleased with herself.

Jive? Rock and roll? The very words are tragic. "Look, Nan," I say. "I can't do that sort of dance in the competition. It needs to be more like what you see in music videos."

"But that's *pornographic*, Beatrice. I should know. Anyway, you said yourself, you're allowed to do *any* style of dance." I am speechless, partly because I'm horrified, and partly because I'm still trying to blow up the airbed. "So it's decided then. You'll do a nice jive dance for your competition and you won't need to be in a group with those mean girls. When they see you on Thursday, they'll be amazed."

Yes, amazed . . . and delighted. But for none of the reasons Nan thinks. Does she want me to die from humiliation?

"You know, Nan," I say desperately, "lessons are expensive, and I don't think Mum and Dad can afford them."

"My treat, love. Anyway, I get a discount because I made

Lulu and Rockin' Ray's costumes for the National Jive Championships last year."

"But who's going to be my partner?" Surely it won't be Rockin' Ray? "All the people taking part *have* to be under sixteen."

"She knows that. She says he's a lovely young man. Don't worry, you'll meet him tomorrow."

"Tomorrow!" This is terrible . . .

"I've booked you in for your first lesson, straight after school. Now, if you don't mind, dear, I really must get back to my book." And with that Nan arranges herself on my bed, takes a big slurp of gin and tonic and opens up her novel. "Sunset's been lured into a hayloft by a wicked millionaire and I can't imagine what's going to happen next!"

2.

"I'm sorryass aboutass the dance-ass," says Kat, doing her puppy eyes at me from our usual bus seat. After a moment's hesitation, I sit down next to her. I manage to be frosty for about 0.25 seconds before she sticks some chocolate under my nose and says, "Twixass?"

Twixass . . . that's funny. I can't stop myself from laughing. We invented the language of "ass" together. It's definitely easier to learn than French.

"I forgive you-ass, Katass," I say, taking the Twix. Then, to seal the deal, we play our bus game. It's good today. At each stop we say a random number and the person who gets on the bus matching that number is our secret lover. I get Sniffin' Jake (who once sniffed my hair in the lunch line) and Kat gets Pearl (*how* appropriate).

When we get to homeroom, she squeezes my arm and says, "Back in a minute," before heading across the room. This morning, Pearl is busy instructing her followers in the ancient art of eyebrow plucking. Kat joins the group of girls who surround her.

I go over to Betty, who's drawing on Amber's arm. Betty's crazy as a badger and I love hanging out with her, but I secretly suspect she finds me boring and only puts up with me because of our girl-gang past. Betty was the fourth member of the Ladybirds. Right now, she's using a red pen to carefully color in a pair of pouting lips, and in the middle of the lips she's written "The Panty Liners" in bubble writing. "Hey, Bea! What d'you think?"

"It's impressive, especially the shading. And it's so big!"

She grins. She looks particularly crazy today, but in a good way, with her raccoon hat, black-rimmed glasses (she doesn't need them, but she thinks they make her look "like a sexy news anchor") and her knee-high socks. No way will Mr. Simms let her get away with all that, but she doesn't care. "It's our dance group's name and logo."

"Really? *You're* entering *Starwars*?"

"Yeah, me, Charlie and Amber are going to be doing some amazing street dancing." She starts to bust some moves to show me what she means. "Just like The Pink Ladies, we're going to be shakin' our booties and jigglin' our jugs in the judges' faces for five minutes . . . but we're going to be doing it *Betty*-style!"

"Ohh," I say, the penny slowly dropping, "so you're going to copy Pearl's group?" Is she insane? Yes, slightly.

"Kind of! Except instead of hot pants—I'm guessing they'll be in hot pants—we'll be dancing in baggy hiking shorts . . . and 'Total Support Front Fastening' bras."

"You've already got them, haven't you?"

"Already *wearing* them! And we won't dance to 'Do Ya Thang' or 'Twang My Thang' or whatever, we're going to have 'When I'm Sixty-Four' by the Beatles. I feel a tiny bit bad about that—I don't want to disrespect the Beatles, or old people, but it'll be totally worth it. It's going to be *massive*, Bea." Her eyes go dreamy as she imagines it, then she flashes them back on to me. "So, big invitation . . . drum roll . . ." She taps her hands on the desk. "Do *you* want to join us?"

For a moment, my heart leaps at the thought of all the fun I could have, but if I did that I'd lose Kat forever. "I'd better not. Kat would never speak to me again. She's in Pearl's 'Twang My Thang' group."

"OMG! You wouldn't want to upset Kat . . . can you imagine?" She laughs, then stops when she sees my face. "What's wrong?"

I consider telling her about Kat dumping me, but decide not to. To see Kat and Betty together, you'd never believe they once made up one half of the Ladybirds. Really, it was their fight that eventually led to our big split.

Just before our nativity play in fourth grade, Betty ripped off her star costume in front of Miss Hooker and screamed "I'm Mary!" again and again and again until her words came true. You see, Betty's mum died when she was tiny and Miss Hooker always felt sorry for her. Unfortunately, Kat was Mary. Chances are they would have forgotten about it by home-time if Kat hadn't snatched Jesus back mid-performance and started the infamous Ladybirds fight.

I don't want to open old wounds. "My nan's come to stay at our house for a few weeks," I say. "She's sleeping in my bedroom . . . with me. We're sharing."

"Are you serious? I wouldn't let *anyone* share my bedroom."

Charlie adds, "No one would *want* to. It's disgusting."

"True."

Suddenly, a shadow looms over us. Pearl is standing, hands on hips, glaring at Betty. She's breathing heavily through her nose in an attempt to look hard and scary. It works. "What are you doing?"

Betty looks up. "What?" Nothing scares Betty. Not even Pearl.

"That." Pearl prods Amber's arm.

"Since you ask *so* nicely, Pearl, I'll explain. I am coloring in a pair of lips. In the center of the lips are the words *The Panty Liners*, which is the name of our, like, totally awesome dance group!"

"You stole our name," says Pearl.

"You're called the Panty Liners too? No way!"

"You know what I mean, weirdo. We're called The Pink Ladies and your name sounds just like ours."

Betty pretends to think about this for a moment. "I don't think it sounds *just* like yours. Really, it's only the first letters that are the same, creating the *illusion* that they're similar." She turns away from Pearl and carries on with her coloring in.

"Change it," says Pearl threateningly.

"Ummm . . . let me think about that . . ." Betty taps her pen on her teeth. "How about . . . no?"

"You think you're so clever, you and your strange little freak friends, don't you?"

Betty ignores Pearl and her "strange little freak friends" all do the same. Everyone can tell when Pearl's about to get nasty. She puts her face close to Betty's.

"You've even got a weird face. It gives me the creeps. You should try some makeup because at the moment your face makes me feel sick. It's bad enough that you smell without having to look at *that*." Pearl presses a finger into Betty's forehead, then turns and walks back to her seat.

Pearl knows just how to hurt someone. Once, *just once*,

Betty forgot to wash the contents of her gym bag and it smelled. Pearl noticed and she's *never* shut up about it since. That's what she's like.

We sit in silence for a few seconds and then Betty says, "And your face looks like a great big pile of steaming—"

"Betty," warns Amber. "She's watching."

"Kat hangs out with such nice people," says Betty, turning to me. Her voice has the whisper of a tremble in it.

"Kat didn't say anything," I say.

Betty looks at me for a moment longer, then turns back to Amber and her tattoo. If Betty and Kat were a Venn diagram, I'd be the squashed bit in the middle.

The rest of the day drags on and after school I leave on my own. Kat's going to Pearl's house to "plan their image," but says she'll call me later.

I'm walking across the playground when a familiar voice calls out, "Over here, Bumble Bea!"

Nan! What's she doing *inside* the playground . . . wearing a white cowboy hat . . . and a Topshop fur coat? She's pushing Emma in her stroller and, for once, my sister looks like the normal one . . . even though her face is painted like a frog.

"Ready for your lesson?" asks Nan.

"Got your bra," says Emma.

"What?" She's got Nan to dress her in green so she looks more frog-like. She's even got little froggy ears—cute.

"Got your BRA on my HEAD!" Emma screams. I hear some sophomore girls gasp. I peer closer. Those aren't ears! Those padded cups belong to the "jazzy" lime-green bra Nan got me for Christmas.

I grab Emma's stroller and jog with her towards the exit. "Come on, Nan," I say, praying she's following me. "I can't be late for my first salsa lesson."

"*Jive* lesson, Bea."

"Yep, jive lesson. Definitely can't be late for that."

Twenty minutes later, we're standing outside a church hall on a deserted street behind Tesco's. Stuck on the information board is a cream flyer for the Memphis Belle Jive Studio. This, combined with the loud rock 'n' roll that's drifting out of the door—something about a "big ol' lovin' machine"—tells me we're at the right place.

I feel sick. Shyness overwhelms me and I'm rooted to the pavement. I *have* to get out of this. Just as I'm thinking about pretending to faint, Nan pushes open the door and disappears inside, dragging Emma behind her.

I can't pretend-faint on my own. It'd be more embarrassing than not fainting at all. So, heart thudding to the music, I push open the door and step inside. The door slams, blocking out the sunlight, and for a moment my eyes can't adjust. Then I see movement in the center of the room.

It's a dance.

A breathtaking dance.

Whirling round the hall are a man and a woman—Lulu and Ray, I guess—and they're dancing so quickly, so *amazingly*, that I just have to smile. Lulu swings in our direction and flashes us an enormous grin. Her red lipstick matches both her Converse and the cherries on her top. Ray, the man spinning her in a never-ending sequence of twists, is best described as Elvis-like, but think lean, mean Elvis, not chubby, forty-deep-fried-squirrel-burgers-a-day Elvis. And my biggest surprise is their age—they're in their twenties, not drawing their pensions as I'd suspected.

Still they keep dancing, slowing down for a few moments to waltz with exaggerated slowness before flying apart again. Bang on the end of the song, Ray swings Lulu up and over his head so she's left upside down, dangling in space. Carefully, he returns her to the ground and they come over to us. I notice that I'm still smiling and all thoughts of pretend-fainting have vanished.

"So you're the Beatrice I've been hearing so much about," says Lulu. "Do you want to learn to jive?"

That's when it hits me. There is *nothing* in the world I want to do more than learn to jive. But even as I consider the incredible possibility that, one day, I could dance like Lulu, I hear myself saying, "Yes, but I could never do what you just did. I can't dance."

"Have you ever tried to dance like this?" she asks.

"No," I admit.

"Then how do you know you can't do it?"

I shrug.

Nan speaks up. "She's right, love. Jive is a different kettle of fish to the stuff you usually do. For one thing, you don't do it on your own. You have a partner and he shows you what to do by leading you."

"It's the men who do all the hard parts," says Ray.

Lulu rolls her eyes. "We won our first jive competition after we'd been dancing together for just two months. You might be a natural. Anyway, Bea, I know you'll be fine because I've found you a great partner. You'll be perfect together."

"Oh," I say in a little voice. Until this moment, I was so distracted by their dancing that I'd forgotten about *Star-wars*. The word *partner* means *boy*, which means my ability to behave like a normal human being will vanish.

Lulu reads my thoughts. "Don't worry. I promise he'll be nice. He has to be . . . He's my brother. I'll beat him up if he isn't perfectly lovely to you." I hear the door at the back of the hall open. "Here he is now!"

We all turn round and watch as a boy-shaped silhouette

walks in. Gradually, this silhouette steps out of the shadows and turns into . . . The Hug!

"Ollie," I whisper, in shock. This is awful . . . this is amazing . . . but most of all, for me, this is *terrifying*. Kat would be in heaven. Even Pearl would jive if it gave her the chance to get close to Ollie Mathews.

"Hi, Bean," he says, dropping his backpack and pulling out his earphones.

"You know who I am!" Now *that* was supposed to stay in my head.

"Well, we go to the same school, get the same bus . . . Plus, I saved your Barbie's life today." At the mention of the word *Barbie*, Emma begins to scream, "Barbiebarbie-barbiebarbie!" like an ambulance siren, gradually changing it to "Bra-Bea, bra-Bea, bra-Bea!" She obviously hasn't forgiven me for taking it off her. Luckily, Nan decides this is a good moment to take her off to buy some chocolate.

"Come on," says Lulu. "You two have got some work to do. Ollie knows a bit so we'll spend today helping Bea catch up. Right, Bea, stand here and, Ollie, stand opposite. Now, hold hands."

No. Way.

What if my hands feel dry? Or, worse, sweaty? What if they just feel weird? Could I have weird hands? The more I think about my hands the weirder they seem. Could I . . . could I possibly have man-hands? I begin to feel sweat squeezing out of my big manly fingertips. Then I think about something more prominent than my hands: my face. Ollie will be staring at my face and he'll see that zit I found this morning on my chin, one of those painful stealth-zits that sits there under your skin, secretly changing the shape of your face until the next time you look in the mirror you've developed a butt-chin. Oh, God, any minute now, Ollie Matthews will be holding hands with a butt-chinned, sweaty, man-handed freak . . . and, what's worse, he *has* to because his sister *made* him.

"Butt chin," I whisper.

"What?" he says.

Then I realize I'm already holding hands with Ollie Matthews and he hasn't screamed or run out of the room. In fact, he's doing what I should be doing: watching Ray and Lulu show us our first move. But for some reason I can't make my eyes behave and they keep sliding, out of control, back to Ollie's as I try to work out what he's doing in this dingy church hall holding hands with Bea "The Wrong Shape" Hogg.

"Concentrate, Bean," he whispers. Just then, Lulu starts issuing complex instructions about "kangaroo hands" and "push turns" and that's the moment I forget who Ollie Matthews is, and start to jive.

And guess what . . . *I can do it.* Each move seems natural and simple. I don't have to screw up my face in concentration and my hands and feet know what they're doing before Lulu even speaks. I can dance. Or, at least, I can *jive* and as far as I'm concerned, as of today, jive *is* dance.

Our lesson lasts two hours, but it feels like twenty minutes. Lulu and Ray show us a move, we copy it, then Ray puts on some music for us to practice to.

By the end of the lesson, I can

1. spin
2. spin under Ollie's arm
3. spin round Ollie's arm
4. spin away from Ollie's arm
5. make eye contact with Ollie's arm and, occasionally, even his face!

It may not sound like much, but, when you put it all together, it feels *incredible* . . . especially the last one. "Right, you two," says Lulu. "That's enough for today. We'll finish with a practice dance. Do you think 'Zoom Zoom Zoom' is too fast, Ray?"

"They'll cope."

And it is fast. Lulu doesn't tell us what to do, Ollie leads and I follow. For the first time that afternoon, it doesn't feel as if we're learning to dance—it feels as if we *are* dancing. Then, almost as soon as it's begun, the music stops.

Nan and Emma, who must have crept in, give us a clap. We're gasping for breath and, as we let go of each other's hands, Ollie falls laughing to the floor. "She's killed me!"

"Don't be silly, Ollie," says Lulu, pulling him up. "I want you both back here same time tomorrow and basically every night after school until the auditions next week." I glance over at Ollie. *Surely* he must want to get out of this? Didn't he only come along in the first place as some weird favor for his sister?

"OK," he says, shrugging.

"Really?" I ask.

"If we don't practice, then Thursday will be a disaster."

"No, I mean, I don't mind coming, but do *you* want to practice tomorrow?"

"Yeah, well, you can't do it without me, can you?"

"No, I suppose not—"

"Right, I've got to go. Mum's picking me up." And with that he grabs his bag, makes a face at Emma (to be fair, she is making one at him) and leaves the hall.

A few minutes later, we leave too.

"Who that rude man?" asks Emma.

As Nan drives us home, I think over the last two hours. One moment, I'm stupidly happy, the next I'm filled with shame. It wasn't as terrifying as I thought it would be, but that was mainly because of Ollie, who, as Nan says, "*is clearly a gentleman.*" There's one particular thing about him that I can't stop thinking about—the shape of his shoulders and arms in his T-shirt. There was something just so, well, *right* about the way it looked.

What's the matter with me? Do I suddenly have a shoulder fetish? When Kat asks me if I think some singer has a "godly bod," I say yes to keep her happy . . . and because I know that any normal fourteen-year-old girl *should* think he's got a godly bod. Really, I feel nothing . . . and this kind of worries me. Kat's *lush* actors and singers look plastic to me, like Emma's paddling pool, all inflated and horrible to touch. Even my "I love Robert Pattinson" thing is invented.

But Ollie in that T-shirt . . . I'd like to rest my head on his shoulder and shut my eyes. I blush at the thought and instead have to rest my burning cheek on the cold window. "Lulu says that tomorrow she's going to teach you the close hold," says Nan.

Whoa. "What's that?" I ask in a faint voice.

"Well, it's what that name suggests: a *close* hold. You rest your arm on your partner's shoulder and he puts his hand on the small of your back. Then you hold hands. It looks a bit like a waltz, but it's much, much closer. Really, your whole bodies are touching from your chest down to your thighs. You just *melt* together."

Oh. My. God.

I allow myself a secret, amazed smile.

Out of the window, I watch houses flash past, their orange windows glowing in the evening light, and I glow too. I glow from the magic of the past two hours and from knowing that tomorrow I will be *melting* in Ollie Matthews's arms.

3.

When I wake up, my glow has vanished and all I'm left with is stomach-knotting fear.

I'm certain that when Ollie sees me on the bus, in the cold light of day, surrounded by his rugby friends, he'll be filled with horror. I held hands with *her*? Getting dressed in the dark, trying not to wake Nan, I even consider telling Mum I'm ill. The thought of seeing him makes me so embarrassed that when I walk into the kitchen I'm already blushing.

"Bea red," says Emma from her position on the potty. She says it, sings it and then writes it in magnets on the fridge. Mum has to help with this.

Trying to build up a bit of confidence, I do something

different with my hair. Emma gave me this giant daisy hair clip for Christmas. I love it because she chose it and it looks like something a Mr. Man would wear. Usually, I clip it in my hair, look in the mirror, wear it round the house, but then put it away. But today I need to do something brave. So instead of spending half an hour straightening my hair and tying it back, I let it go "au naturel" (my hair is so curly that, left to its own devices, it goes beyond natural and slips into the *super*natural). I push the daisy hair clip behind my ear into a tangle of curls.

"Ohh," says Emma as I leave the house. "Bea pretty!"

When I get on the bus, Kat isn't there and in a panic I sit next to Bus Kelly. She's this teeny seventh-grade girl who is so desperate for friends she's frightened everyone off. Usually she sits on her own . . . but not today. She grins and I quickly call Kat before Kelly can speak to me.

No answer. This is so strange. How could Kat abandon me in my hour of need? When I got in last night, I texted her with the most amazing gossip of my life: **Hey K guess what? am entering comp with ollie matthews OLLIE MATTHEWS!!! omgomgomg :-D xx Bean.** But she didn't text or ring back like I was expecting.

Yesterday, I didn't pay much attention because I was on a jive-high, showing Mum films of Lulu and Ray on

YouTube and getting Nan to do a demo with me to "Jailhouse Rock." Swinging under Nan's arm was difficult because she has the dimensions of a jacket potato—small and round—but Mum got the idea. In the end, all four of us were dancing around the living room with Emma yelling, "Watch me chive! Watch me chive!"

I'm brought out of my jive-dream by Bus Kelly tugging my sleeve. "You're Bea, aren't you?" she says. I nod. "You look funny. What's wrong?"

"I feel sick." Can I ask Bus Kelly to look down the bus and see if Ollie is there? I *really* need Kat and her little mirror. Where is she?

The bus pulls up at the stop before school and a load of sophomores pile off. They push down the aisle and that's when I hear Ollie talking to his mates. "Seriously," he says, "they taste good. Try one." I start to panic. I must appear occupied. In a moment of desperation I ask Bus Kelly who her favorite teacher is. Just as she opens her mouth to reply, Ollie is standing next to me saying, "One for Bea," and shoving a packet of sweets under my nose, "and don't let the name put you off."

Obediently, I take a sweet and glance at the packet. I read, "Sick 'n' Mix."

"Carrot chunk," I say as I stick the lurid orange sweet in my mouth.

He carries on down the bus, passing out his gross sweets and that's it. Mission accomplished. I spoke to

Ollie. *He* spoke to me! Admittedly, all I said was "carrot chunk" but, hey, it's a start. I sit there smiling, thinking, It's going to be alright . . . It's all going to be alright!

Whack! A bag smacks me on the back of my head and I fly forward, hitting my forehead on the seat in front. My hair's messed up and the daisy clip falls to the floor. I look up. Pearl is standing there, holding up the line.

Not taking her eyes off me, she moves her face close to mine and whispers, "Bitch." Her breath is an odd combination of cigarettes and mint. My stomach melts and the little kids around me gasp, getting ready for a fight, but Pearl just pushes past everyone.

Bus Kelly tugs at my blazer. "You're dead, Bea."

I know it.

It's only when I get off the bus at school that I realize something amazing has happened. I didn't cry. The scariest girl in the school thinks I'm a bitch, but I *didn't cry.*

As I walk into study hall, I finally hear from Kat: **Sorry not on bus. Bton 4 dentists lol!!** Whenever Kat's mum wants to take her shopping in Brighton, she says Kat has a dentist appointment. Kat's had five "dentist" appointments so far this year.

Realizing I'm friendless, I sit down next to Betty. "Hello, bitch," she says, cheerfully.

"Good news travels fast."

"Amber's brother was sitting behind you on the bus. What did you do?"

"Well, Pearl hasn't told me, but I guess it has something to do with me entering *Starwars* with Ollie Matthews."

Betty's mouth drops open. "No. Way. Seriously? NO WAY!" She slams her hand down on the desk and roars with laughter. "Charlie, Amber!" The girls have just walked in. "Get ready for the most bizarre news ever: Our very own, little, lovely, *quiet* Bea Hogg is entering *Starwars* with . . . you're never going to believe this . . . Ollie *McFittie* Matthews!"

"No!" says Charlie.

"That's crazy," says Amber. "How come?"

They gather round me and I explain as quietly as I possibly can. Pearl has come in and is now staring coldly at me, but the girls keep asking me questions and laughing and gasping and asking more questions and then more questions.

"Ah! You're going to be jive bunnies. That's so cool," says Charlie. "Seriously, Bea, he's nice. My brother's friends with him and he's always around our place."

"And, like, not to forget how he's completely and utterly *Beautimus Maximus*," adds Betty. "Did you see him when they did that rugby thing in assembly? He has a seriously gorgeous—"

"Shut up," says Charlie, clamping her hand over Betty's mouth. "You're embarrassing her."

And then I can't resist sharing my born-again jiviness with them. I go into more and more detail about the arm jive (I can do it) and the judo flip (I can't) and I don't care that they're laughing because I'm laughing too. As I'm explaining the intimacy levels of "the yoyo" using two mobile phones, I make the mistake of glancing up and I momentarily lock eyes with Pearl.

"Freak," she says, before turning back to her friends and whispering something that makes them snigger. Suddenly, her phone vibrates. "It's him," she says as she studies the screen. Then, looking at me, she smiles a cold, satisfied smile and my happiness dissolves.

At that moment, I realize two things: (1) someone must have told her about me and Ollie and the likely candidate is Kat; and (2) "him" is totally and obviously Ollie.

"Come on, Bea. What does the Nokia do?" asks Betty.

"Oh, well, that's it really," I say, passing the phones back.

Pearl thinks she's in competition with me. This is ridiculous! It's like America declaring war on the Isle of Wight. And, just to clarify, Pearl is the world superpower and I'm the island selling cream teas.

I finally catch up with Kat in French. Appropriately, her nails have a very professional-looking French polish and I'm fairly certain her shoes are new. "*Regardez mes nouvelles chaussures!*" she whispers.

Yep. I try to be cold, but that's difficult because

Mr. Tweed produces a fruit bowl from under his desk and starts throwing oranges around the room, instructing us to role-play fruit shopping with our partners. Kat's my partner. I can't ignore her because she keeps saying "*Voulez-vous une* pear?" and juggling two big imaginary boobies.

She does this continuously until I start to laugh. After an awkward pause, I relent and ask her how The Pink Ladies' dance is coming along. She describes every detail of their hip swivels and sassy krumps—which I initially mistake for some of her mum's yummy Swedish biscuits—and then she moves on to telling me how *friendly* Pearl is, not evil like I think at all, just really *fun* and *ordinary*, just like in the Ladybird days. "So," she says finally, "*you* and Ollie Matthews!"

"You got my text?"

"Only this morning. I had my phone turned off last night and, oh, sorry about the bus. Mum just had to get to the French Connection sale and wanted an opinion on some harem pants," she babbles nervously, not making total sense. "My opinion was *totally puke*, but I said they were awesome so she'd buy me the shoes. Anyways . . . you and Ollie, how did *that* happen?"

I explain my nan's plan and my surprise at the dance class. Finally, I have the courage to ask, "Did you hear what Pearl said on the bus?" She nods. "Did you tell her about me and Ollie?"

Kat does her silly-old-ditsy-old-me face that gets her out of most situations. "I just didn't think it was a big deal, Bea. I was chatting on the phone about who was entering with who and it kind of slipped out."

I thought she'd turned her phone off. She had time to talk to Pearl and gossip about *Starwars*, but couldn't reply to my text? I feel slightly sick.

"Bean," says Kat, "as your best friend, I've got to say I really don't think you should dance with Ollie."

"Why not?"

"He's practically Pearl's boyfriend and she's mad at you. And, you know, she likes getting her own way." Kat smiles as though everything's the same as usual and we're just gossiping about what a lunatic Pearl turned into.

"Are they going out?" I ask, putting as much casual nonchalance into my voice as I can.

"Practically. She's taking it slow. Doesn't want to rush things." My heart sinks. "When's your next rehearsal?"

Looking down at my orange, I try to accept what Kat's just told me. "We're meeting straight after school."

"Right, you see, Pearl just told me she got a text from Ollie and he wants to meet *her* after school. I thought you should know. I don't want you to feel bad when he doesn't show up." She squeezes my arm. "Maybe he's not as great as we thought he was."

And then Mr. Tweed starts to ask us questions about

the color of cars and I realize I may not have been concentrating a hundred percent on the lesson.

Throughout the rest of the day, I get little comments and cold stares whenever I see Pearl. I do my best to avoid her, walking elaborate routes to classes and hiding in the library at lunchtime, but at the end of the day, when I'm stuffing some books in my locker, I look up to discover her leaning against the lockers, watching me. She's alone.

"I'm meeting my boyfriend here," she says. "Did you come to watch?" She moves closer as I shut my locker. "I said, *Did you come to watch?*" I try to step round her, but she keeps blocking my path until I'm doing this pathetic dance. On either side of us, students stand and stare.

Suddenly, she stops moving and I squeeze past. Fighting the urge to run, I walk down the corridor, and above the sound of slamming lockers and cries of "bye" I can hear her laughing. The sound follows me as I rush down the stairs and out of school.

Nan's waiting in the car as instructed.

"Looking forward to the lesson, love?" she asks as I put on my seat belt.

And that is all it takes. Just *one* person being nice to me. "Quick, Nan, drive," I whisper between sobs as I pretend to look for a Life Saver in the glove compartment.

"Shush up!" yells Emma from the backseat. "Noisy girl!" And she throws her Shrek doll at me. He repeats,

"Better out than in!" and only stops when I slam him again and again on the dashboard, which is hard to do when you're trying to hide.

Now Emma's screaming too.

When we're a couple of roads away from school, I sit up and, still hiccupping and wiping snot and tears from my face, I explain that, "There's *no point* going to the lesson because Ollie's not going to be there. He's going to be kissing a *horrible* girl with no eyebrows and *massive boobs*, and clearly this is what he'd *rather* be doing than *jiving* with me, so I won't go to the dance studio because it will be the humiliating cherry on the cake of a very humiliating cake day!" I get a bit confused at the end.

"But you've got very impressive bosoms, Bea," says Nan.

"Not impressive enough!"

"Come on, dear. Give him the benefit of the doubt. What if those girls made it all up and he arrives only to find out that you're not there? Look, we're here now so we might as well go in."

And so, too tired and fed up to argue, I get lured into the Memphis Belle Jive Studio for the second day in a row.

In the toilets, I wash my face and splash water on my eyes. Next, I set to work with baby wipes, Marc Jacobs's Daisy Sunshine (stolen from Mum's dressing table) and Dove Maximum Protection. I'm taking no chances. I sniff myself all over—even my hands—and then I realize I've made myself smell like a weird combination of Mum and Emma, so I rub off the perfume with more baby wipes until I just smell like Emma.

I check my appearance in the mirror. Well, I look short as usual, but at least you can't tell I've been crying. I'm wearing my one and only nice pair of jeans, my favorite faded T-shirt that Dad got me from America and my daisy clip. I pull on my old school shoes, which have a slight heel because Lulu says I can't wear flat shoes or sneakers as they'll stop me from spinning. Not bad, I think, for a small, wrong-shaped person with cloud-hair. Taking a deep breath, I push open the door.

No Ollie.

Of course no Ollie. What was I expecting?

Lulu notices me hovering by the door and beckons me in. "C'mon. He's just late. We'll start without him."

Nan catches my eye and smiles.

"Now, we're going to start with the close hold. Ray, you show Bea where her hands need to be." It looks like I'm going to be dancing with Rockin' Ray, after all. Mind you, now that I've met him it's not so bad.

"Sorry about this, Bea," says Ray, "but we've got to get *very* close for this dance to work." And with that he clutches me to his entire right-hand side so we are touching from shoulder to hip. Squeezed against his chest, I can smell his roll-up cigarettes and feel the warmth of his body. Kat would die to see me right now. "I sort of control the dance with my hand that I place on the small of your back. Do you see?"

He shows me how he will steer me from left to right with the pressure of his hand. Lulu puts on "In the Mood" and, after a couple more instructions, we're off, properly dancing.

My worries slip from my mind as Ray leads me. It's easy to respond to the signals of his hands, and instinctively I know when to turn and when to spin away. He's an incredible dancer and soon I feel like a film star in a black-and-white movie. My back straightens and my chin rises and I feel Shy Bea disappearing. Then the dance is ending, and Ray swings me around twice, very quickly.

"You're a natural, Bea," he says. "Now try it with Ollie."

And that's when I realize he's sitting up on the stage watching me.

We stand opposite each other and assume the close hold. I don't feel like a movie star anymore. I feel more like a great big doofus who smells like a baby. But, just like yesterday, Ollie is serious and businesslike, following Lulu's instructions with care, and after a few practice dances we seem to be mastering the close hold. I try not to enjoy it too much and keep reminding myself that Ollie was late because he was enjoying an even closer hold with Pearl.

We're in the middle of a dance when Lulu turns the music off. We freeze in position. "It's not right," she says. "You just aren't getting *close* enough. Ollie, imagine you are *glued* to Bea and you have to dance like one person."

Ollie frowns and looks at how we are standing.

Yes, we're close, embarrassingly ultra-close, but there's still about ten centimeters between us. We shuffle closer. Now there's five centimeters between us. "Oh, c'mon," says Lulu, putting her hands on our hips and pushing us together so that our sides touch. Now my face is brushing against Ollie's T-shirt. I look up at him. This is ridiculous. My cheeks begin to burn.

"Hello," he says. "Hey, nice T-shirt. 'Hill Valley High School.' That's from *Back to the Future*!"

"You like it?" He is literally the *only* other person my age who has ever heard of this movie.

"Like it? I'm almost wearing it."

I laugh. "I meant the movie . . ."

"I know. Hey, sorry I was late—"

"It's OK," I cut in. I don't want to hear him say *her* name.

Suddenly, the music starts and this time we stick close together. Ollie leads, altering the pace so that one minute we're flying and the next we're slowing down. The feel of his shoulder under my hand is the *best* thing, strong and warm, better even than when I put my hand on Emma's back when she's asleep.

And all of a sudden, the "L" word comes into my head. I *love* putting my hand on Emma's back. I *love* resting my hand on Ollie's shoulder . . . I *love* Ollie Matthews's shoulder!

My heart pounds. No one can *ever* know.

It would ruin everything!

The music stops and we spring apart. I turn to Lulu for our next instructions, knowing that if Ollie looks at me he'll see my shoulder-love written all over my face.

"Brilliant, you two. Great!" Lulu's thrilled. Slowly, my heart returns to its normal speed. "Right, I've got an idea to get you ready for the audition. Every Saturday, Ray and I host a jive night in Brighton. We've got a live band this weekend and, if you come along, you'll get to see some amazing dancing. What do you think? Are you busy?" She looks at me.

Honestly? I *am* kind of busy. I'm the youngest member (by sixty years) of the Silver Stitchers, Nan's quilting club, and on Saturday evenings we watch *X Factor* and get stitching. Really, I just mix the drinks—they like them strong—and thread needles . . . but I think the Stitchers can do without me for one night.

"If I rearrange something, I can make it," I say.

"Cool," says Ollie. "I'm not busy."

Interesting.

"I'll pick you up at six, and, Ollie"—Lulu gives him a look—"don't be late!"

After Ollie has left, I walk to the car.

I notice that the sky is in that magic in-between time when there's still a glimmer of sunlight left. Dad told me it's called "the gloaming," which is a sad word for something so beautiful. The houses around the hall are silhouetted, and somewhere above me a blackbird sings. For once, Nan and Emma aren't chattering.

Pushing aside all the questions that are swirling around my head, I enjoy the twilight. Who cares what happens at school tomorrow? Right now, I have a starring role in my life . . . and I love it!

4
♡

On Wednesday, I find fries in my math book, Thursday sees me tripped up in the cafeteria and Friday begins with a panty liner stuck to my locker. At first I think this is some obscure message from The Panty Liners, but on closer examination I see someone has written "Bea Hogg smells" on it. Probably not Betty then. Nothing really bad happens if Kat's hanging with Pearl, but she never comes over to talk to me. I peel off the panty liner and stuff it in the nearest garbage. Right now, dazzling spins and hot shoulders seem like a distant dream. I cling to the thought of Saturday, when I will spend the whole evening dancing with Ollie.

For the rest of the day, I try to stick close to Betty, but

at lunchtime I manage to get pasta flicked at me from an upstairs window. For this, I get a rare text from Kat: **Bea big hugs saw pasta in hair : (if i talk to u P says no pink ladies xxx.** I go to the bathroom to wash out the tomato and basil sauce.

While I'm there, I go into a stall and I'm just about to hover over the chipped seat when a fist slams hard into the door, followed by a kick. Next, the cubicle's being smacked on all sides. I yank up my tights and the thumping and banging stops.

Silence.

I hold my breath, waiting to see if they're gone. Laughter bursts out above my head and I look up to see a hand holding a phone over the top of the cubicle and then I her a click. I feel sick and I actually begin to tremble . . .

"Leave my boyfriend alone, rat," says a familiar voice. Then the door slams once more and they're gone.

I'm still shaking when I find Betty in homeroom.

"Seriously, Bea, you've *got* to do something," she says after I explain how close I came to being humiliated on Facebook. "Pearl won't stop until *you* make her stop."

"She'll leave me alone the second I stop dancing with Ollie." I scribble a twisty flower on the back of my hand.

"Will you do that?"

"No."

"Well, remember what Miss Cherry taught us at Lady-birds?" I shake my head. "One, put your hand up and say, 'Stop it. I don't like it.' Have you tried that?"

"No. She'd bite my hand."

"That's possible. Two, tell a teacher."

"No. She thrives on a challenge. That will just make her think of more evil things to do, but stuff that no one can pin on her."

Betty has started to add some leaves to my flower. "Looks like it's number three then . . ."

"What's that?"

"Karate-chop her, or call her something really offensive."

"I don't remember Miss Cherry saying that one."

"It's the most fun. I can't see you karate-chopping Pearl so you need to say something rude, anything, just so she knows you're not scared."

"But I *am* scared!"

"I know, but it's like acting. You start by pretending, then it sort of takes over and becomes true. Let's practice. I'm Pearl, you're Bea." Betty piles her hair on top of her head, sucks in her cheeks and scowls. But we just laugh. "OK, I'm doing it for real this time. Ready?" I nod. "Look, you weirdo freak, just leave Ollie Matthews alone. He's my man muffin and you know it!"

"I do, I do. I'm so sorry!" I hide behind my book.

"No! Try again . . ."

"Right." I take a deep breath. "Don't you *ever* tell me what to do, Mr. . . . . *Poo Head!*"

Betty collapses. "Yes, she is a Mr. Poo Head, but you aren't fighting a toddler. If you ever say that to her, please make sure I'm around to watch. It'll be epic."

But, of course, I don't say or do anything. Instead, I keep my head down, try to avoid Mr. Poo Head, and dream of Saturday night . . . a whole night spent dancing in the arms of Ollie Matthews. The idea is bliss, even if a nagging voice at the back of my head keeps saying, *But why would he ever want to spend Saturday night with* you?

"They'll be here soon!" says Nan, peering around the curtains.

She just got back from a shopping trip and found me perched on the edge of the sofa, watching *Dirty Dancing* and checking the time every few minutes. The second Emma's released from her stroller, she crouches down, frowns and begins to jiggle in time to "She's Like the Wind." This is how she always dances and she can keep it up for hours. Hopefully, she'll develop a few more moves before she hits her teens.

"We got you a surprise!" Nan hands me a rectangular box.

I peel away several layers of pink tissue paper and see

a pair of shoes. They're made of the softest leather ever, and the front is pleated to form a flower over the toes. They are gorgeous, but they are red. And I mean bright, shouting RED.

"Do you like them?"

"I love them . . . but they're very . . . red." I hold them in my hands.

"Try them on."

So I do and, of course, they fit perfectly.

"I've never worn red shoes before," I say. "They sort of stand out, don't they?"

"What's wrong with that? Red shoes are the best shoes. Every girl should have a pair. Now, I know you love to cover yourself from head to foot in black or gray, but if you like them, wear them. Remember: *Though she be but little . . .*"

"*. . . she is fierce,*" I say, but without much enthusiasm. Nan once played Helena in her school production of *A Midsummer Night's Dream* and this is the one line she remembers. When I was little, she'd repeat it to me to give me courage, like if I wanted to pet a big dog or go down a slide on my own.

"Shakespeare knows what he's talking about, Beatrice."

Just then, the doorbell rings and I'm kissing Emma good night (after she demands a "Big wet one, please!"), running down the path and slipping into the back of Lulu's car.

"Cool shoes," says Ollie as we pull away from the curb.

Thank you, Shakespeare! I settle back into my seat and run my hands over the cream leather. "Isn't she beautiful?" says Lulu. "You are sitting in a baby-blue Chevrolet Bel Air and one of only four in the country." I notice a couple of boys have stopped their bikes in the middle of the road to stare at Lulu. With her blond waves and red bow lips, she looks like Marilyn Monroe.

"This is the best thing I've ever sat on," I say, wriggling in my seat. "Except maybe Darth Vader's lap. That was good, but scary . . . he was doing the voice."

"*The* Darth Vader?" asks Ollie.

"I was eight," I say, as if this explains it all, and then I shut up because I suddenly realize that heading off into the night with Ollie Matthews is far scarier than sitting on Darth Vader's lap.

We drive through our deserted High Street, across the downs and arrive in Brighton as the sun is setting. Lulu's car continues to draw stares as we head along the seafront. Strings of white lights sway between lampposts, glittering against the dark sky.

We pull up outside a shabby cream building and I follow Lulu and Ollie through a dark lobby and into a vast dance hall. Slowly, I turn around, trying to take in the high ceiling and the elegant white pillars that line the gleaming dance floor.

"Come on, Bea," says Lulu, heading towards the stage. "You've got work to do."

We put out three hundred chairs and arrange tea lights on the tables. Ollie drifts off to help DJ Crazy Ray (aka Ray) with the sound equipment. Finally, after Lulu and I have lit the candles, the hall is ready. Before they go off to get changed, Ray puts on some music and Lulu turns off the main lights.

Then Ollie and I are alone.

I sit at the side of the room, struggling to arrange my face and body into a relaxed pose to hide the fact that Shy Bea has *totally* taken over. Meanwhile, Ollie is on the stage fiddling with the lighting. This is stupid. I stand up. *Though she be but little, she is fierce*, I think. *No!* hisses Shy Bea. *Fierce is stupid. Hide in the bathroom!* After a moment's hesitation, I force myself to join Ollie on the stage.

"What're you doing?" I ask, oh so casually.

"I can't get those red lights to work." Ollie absent-mindedly points to the ceiling. "Those ones up there."

"That's because this," I say, pulling out a yellow cable, "needs to be in here," and I push the lead into the top power strip. The red lights came on and circle the room.

Ollie looks at me properly for the first time that evening. "That is the single most impressive thing I have *ever* seen a girl do."

"My dad taught me. He's in a band. Sometimes I help them set up."

"Good skills."

"Thank you." I don't mention that it's a blues band called Dave and the Bearded Weasels. We stand in silence watching the lights swing across the empty dance floor.

The track that's playing changes.

"I love this song," says Ollie, turning up the volume. "Growing up with a sister who's stuck in the fifties has given me unusual music taste." He turns to me. "Do you want to dance? I mean, y'know, to practice?"

"OK," I say.

Ollie jumps off the stage and I go to follow, but he put his hands up to me and I jump straight into his arms. When I land, he swings me into the dance. As the hall is empty, we use the whole dance floor. It starts off as a lazy dance and, as the lights swoop across our faces, I start to relax.

It's nice to be dancing on our own.

Suddenly, the music speeds up and so do we, and even though we make a lot of mistakes, it feels like real dancing. Soon we're dancing faster than ever and it becomes impossible to keep up with each other. The more we get wrong the funnier it gets. Spinning around Ollie's back, I miss his hand and go flying across the hall. As I make my way back towards him, he starts to break-dance (badly) and by the time Lulu and Ray come back, we're spinning around like Jack and Rose in *Titanic* and all my shyness has been danced out of me.

An hour later, the hall is full and a sea of dancers takes up the entire floor. Some of the men are dressed in tailored trousers, suspenders and shirts, others in rolled-up jeans and T-shirts. The women wear exquisite tea dresses, pedal pushers and full skirts in a rainbow of colors. Ollie and I stand at the top of a set of stairs, like swimmers too scared to take the plunge, watching the color and movement that surrounds us. Finally, he grabs my hand and pulls me down the steps.

And I love it. We dance *all* night, stopping occasionally for water, and by the end of the evening we're exhausted, dripping with sweat and limping. Luckily, Nan made me bring Band-Aids and I've used four by the time Ray puts on the final track. It's a slow, slow song and the mood changes completely as all around us couples press together, heads resting on shoulders, hands slipping down backs.

"I need some fresh air," says Ollie, dropping my hand. "Coming?"

We sit on a wall outside the hall, getting our breath back, and watch as people leave, hair slipping out of ponytails, shirts coming untucked. The night air is icy and crisp on my hot skin and, between buildings, I can see a low moon reflecting on the black sea.

"That was the *best* night," I say, not caring how tragic I sound. I glance at Ollie. He's got out his phone.

"Just checking the time," he says, and then there is an awkward silence.

Why is he here, with me, on a Saturday night?

"Do you *really* want to do this?" I blurt out. "I mean, enter the dance competition with *me*? Did Lulu make you do it?"

"Do you think I'd try to get on national TV to help out my sister?" he says. "Plus, she's not even my real sister. She's only a half sister."

"So you want to do this? You're not embarrassed or anything?"

"Embarrassed of what?" He puts away his phone.

"Jiving in front of everyone from school?"

"No."

"Dancing in front of all your friends, the rugby team, all of the tenth grade?"

"Have you ever seen me being embarrassed of anything? Do you remember when I was a white blood cell for the science fair—"

"In the transparent garbage bag?"

". . . and the Speedos, that's the one. Then there was the time I did that Rod Stewart impression in assembly."

"And you did that thrusty thing into Mrs. P's face."

"Yeah." Ollie laughs at the memory.

"And now there's going to be the time you jived with me, Bea Hogg. I don't think it's as funny as those other things you did." Then, a terrible thought strikes me. Could he be doing this to be funny? To make his friends laugh at his latest crazy stunt? My cheeks begin to burn. Ollie looks over.

"I'm doing it because I want to," he says. "I don't think it's a 'sad' dance and I don't care if anyone else does. I'll let you into a secret." He sighs and takes a deep breath. "I want to be an actor and singer, starring in musicals in the West End . . . I'm a little embarrassed about *that*," he adds with a laugh.

"Tonight, ladies and gentlemen," I say in a booming showbiz voice, "Ollie Matthews will be staring as . . . Lumiere!"

"Who's Lumiere?"

"The singing candlestick in *Beauty and the Beast*."

"Yes! That's what I want to do . . . be Lumiere, or any singing object, as long as I get on the stage. I'm going to audition for the National Youth Theatre and study at drama school. Doing this will help me . . . especially if we win."

"Do you really think we can?"

"Well, I doubt anyone else will be jiving. Winning *Starwars* could make all the difference to my chances."

"So you *really* want to do this?"

"Yes. I *really* want to do this."

"Even with me?"

"Yes! Even with *you*," he says. "You're funny, Bea. Come on, we've got a hundred candles to blow out."

I let myself into my house and everyone is asleep. Mum knew I was going to be late. I can't go to bed because my ears are still ringing from the music and my mind is buzzing. I make some hot chocolate, open a pack of oat cookies and then sit on the sofa, smiling to myself, and munching my way through half the pack.

I run through the whole night from start to finish. Then it hits me. I have spent the evening with a member of the opposite sex, talking to him, *touching* him, making him laugh . . . everything.

I am normal.

I am normal!

Then, because I have to hug someone to celebrate having a life and not having to remain a member of the Silver Stitchers forever, I creep into Emma's room and give her a hug. Her eyes flutter open for a second and she says, "Monkey's got the sprinkles."

She must be having a good dream, so I leave her to it.

I slip into my room and climb onto the airbed. Nan sighs and rolls over. Even my snoring roomie can't ruin my mood. I curl up and smile to myself. I am not going to think about *Starwars*, or the fact that dancing with Ollie could end on Thursday. Tonight, I'm floating on air . . . on an airbed . . . with blisters all over my feet. Nan's low nose-whistle soon builds into a full on power-snore. It has no effect on me. I'm simply too happy.

5.

On Monday, I get a nasty surprise on the bus.

Opening a text from an unknown number, I read, **u r a dog :-D.** My heart sinks. Pearl is creeping into every corner of my life. Who gave her my number? Would Kat do that?

"That's cyberbullying," says a little voice, and I look down to see Bus Kelly staring at me with big eyes. I usually sit next to her these days. "Do you know what you should do?"

I'm reluctant to reply. It's unwise to encourage Bus Kelly. If I speak to her I will officially be her best friend. "What should I do?" I ask. I'm beyond caring.

"Send a message back that says, 'I'm gonna mess your face up!'"

I'm fairly certain this isn't official advice so I just go with ignoring it. Messages creep in throughout the day: **yo u ugly fat pig :)**, **u loser :)** and **I hate u rat :D**—you've got to love the smilies—and finally, as I'm going to our rehearsal, I get, **die u plank ;-)** What? Die you *plank*? Hang on . . . I've got it. She means *skank*.

I feel a small sense of satisfaction as I walk up to the Memphis Belle Jive Studio. The one thing Pearl wants me to do is stop dancing with Ollie, but, whoops, look where I am now! I push open the door to find Ollie and Lulu practicing a move. Watching them wipes my mind clear of Pearl's texts.

"Get over here, Bea," says Lulu, the moment they finish. "I've got just three rehearsals to teach you the routine I've choreographed. It's simple, but that means you can learn it fast."

I sit down next to Ollie and watch Lulu and Ray step through the dance. "It builds up to an aerial called the knickerbocker," Lulu calls over her shoulder. "Here it comes!" She leans back into Ray's open arms and then he flips her over in a somersault. She lands with a light bounce making it look so easy. "Right, we'll talk you through it. It's simple."

It isn't. Each time we try, I crash back the way I've come and it just gets worse and worse. I start to think I'm too big to fly over like Lulu, and, as soon as this idea enters my head, it becomes even harder. "Sorry," I say each time. Ollie just shrugs.

"We'll forget it for now," says Lulu, after I've tumbled to the ground for the seventh time. "I was probably being overambitious. If you get through on Thursday, we can add it to the routine."

As I leave the hall, my body aching, my phone beeps. Message from unknown number: **u r fat :-D.** Now all of me aches. I glance around me. The road is empty, except for a few parked cars and a van. A Coke can rolls down the gutter, clattering against the curb.

"Hey!"

I jump and turn round. Lulu's followed me out of the hall. "You OK?" she asks.

"Yeah, just"—I glance down at my phone that I've got clutched tight in my hand—"checking my messages."

"I'm glad I caught you. I forgot to ask, what are you going to wear on Thursday?"

I laugh. I've thought about this a lot, but beyond my lovely red shoes everything I own is totally Shy Bea and the exact opposite of dazzling-teen-dancing-queen. "Jeans and a vest?" I suggest.

She's not impressed. "You need a look that matches the dance. Nothing overdone, something cool, something a bit vintage. Ollie's prepared with a fifties shirt." She looks at me, her eyes narrowed. "Hey, I know, I've got a gorgeous top you can have!"

"What about my hair?" I tug at the end of my cloud of

curls that's being blown about in the wind. After rehearsal, my hair goes extra wild so right now it's pretty out of control.

"D'you know what you need, Bea?" says Lulu. "A makeover!" She claps her hands and jumps up and down. "I'll come round to your place on Thursday and help you get ready. If you like, I can drop you in Brighton too."

As I walk home, the word *audition* echoes round my mind. It is *actually* going to happen. Anxiety washes over me and my stomach executes several perfect knicker-bockers.

Beep, beep, goes my phone.

"Oh, shut up, Mr. Poo Head," I say, stuffing it to the bottom of my bag.

On Thursday, The Pink Ladies are so busy rehearsing and perfecting their look that Pearl gives me the day off—I don't even get any texts. School seems to last forever, but as soon as I'm let out of math I go home and jump in the shower.

I'm toweling my hair when Emma drags Lulu into my room. I'm pleased to see that Emma's wearing her favorite outfit of *nothing at all*. Oh, except for one sock and a crown. She likes to accessorize her nudity.

Lulu starts work immediately. She gets Nan to paint

my nails (bright red) while she applies a toned-down version of her own makeup to my face: lots of black mascara, a wisp of black eyeliner painted on with a tiny brush and matte red lips.

Finished, she holds me at arm's length, but frowns at the overall effect. This does not fill me with confidence.

"Something's not right, Bea," she says, before rolling up my jeans so they become pedal pushers and getting me to put on her top.

It's a skin-tight white cardigan with small pearl buttons and a scoop neck. She won't let me wear anything underneath it, well, except my bra, obviously. Jiving bra-less would be very distracting for all concerned. She unbuttons a couple more buttons on the cardi. I have big boobs. Fact. Usually I do all I can to hide them from the world, but they're pretty assertive. I look down. All I can see is flesh. My flesh.

Can I really stand in front of Ollie like this? My cheeks burn at the thought of him looking at me. Automatically, my hand goes up to the buttons.

"Leave them," says Lulu firmly.

"Don't I look a bit—"

"Amazing? Yes." Lulu smiles. "Bea, do you trust me?"

"Sure, I guess . . . why?"

"I want to cut your hair." We leave in less than half an hour and, as far as I know, Lulu isn't a hairdresser. "Don't worry. I've cut my friends' hair lots of times . . . well, a few times. I don't want to do anything complicated, just take off a couple of inches."

"A couple?"

"Well, about eight."

I think for a second or two. My hair falls well below my shoulders. Not that I ever wear it down. Or, at least, not since Lauren complained that she couldn't see the whiteboard in geography and Miss McCredie moved me to the back.

I'm about to say that cutting my hair is just one scary thing too many to happen today, but then I think, *Why not?* I'm planning on dancing in public, with Ollie Matthews, with my boobs and stomach showing . . . will eight inches of hair make much difference? "OK. You can do it!" Lulu grins and whips out a pair of scissors. "You had this planned all along, didn't you?"

"I've been dying to cut your hair since the day I met you," she says. "Do you know how many women would kill to have hair like yours?" And with that she grabs my hair into a loose ponytail and goes *snip, snip, snip, snip,* cutting the whole lot off.

Nan, who's been sitting on my bed, groans and leaves the room. "I'm sorry, Lulu," she says. "I'm sure you know what you're doing, but I can't watch."

This leaves me with Lulu, the self-taught hairdresser,

and Emma, who's crouched on the floor burying her face in my freshly cut hair and saying, "Look! Emma a mole!"

"Just got to even it out a bit," says Lulu, frowning.

I shut my eyes. "Don't let her eat it, Lulu."

"Found a worm!" Emma cries.

Too late.

6.

Back in Brighton, we cruise along the seafront. The pier still sparkles with flashing lights, like a mini Vegas, but tonight gray clouds are partially covering a blue sky.

I see the queue before I see the Brighton Centre, stretching down the road and around a corner. Hundreds of dancers crowd the pavement. There are dads glancing at watches, mums touching up makeup, and a few coaches in dance-studio sweatshirts.

"Lulu . . . I feel sick."

"I know." She pats my arm. "Just remember to relax your shoulders . . . oh, and when Ollie spins you behind his back make sure you pause for a beat." She slows the car down as we drive down the line. Groups of girls are practicing their routines below posters that advertise mysterious events like Space Invader, Junk Disco and Tiger Tiger and all along the line phones are out and texts and photos are flying around.

Then I spot the cameras.

I didn't realize they would be filming the auditions, but there are three cameras crews wandering up and down the street, making girls scream and strike poses. Suddenly, I see The Panty Liners. "Here's fine, Lulu." Ollie will just have to find me.

"Good luck!" she calls as I jump out of the car. Immediately, two cameras swing in our direction, then follow the Chevrolet's progress down the road. Lulu's slim white arm reaches out of the driver's window and waves as she does a dramatic U-turn and swings out of sight.

But Betty and the girls aren't watching Lulu. They're watching me. I remember my hair. I put my hand up to touch it and it's still as short as it was when we left my house forty minutes ago.

"Bea?" says Betty. "You look *totally* different."

Lulu can't have gotten too far yet. I want to race down the road, jump in her car and yell, "Take me home!" Soon, I could be curled up on the sofa with my sister and Nan, watching *The Simpsons*.

"Different?" I say. "Different terrible or different good?"

"Good!" she says. "I'd forgotten that you've got curly hair . . . and where've you been keeping *them* hidden?" She points at my unbuttoned cardi. "Hi, Bea's boobs. I'm Betty. Pleased to meet you at last!"

To cover my embarrassment I talk like a maniac, barely pausing for breath, telling them all about Lulu's makeover and how I had to pull a hairball out of Emma's mouth. What's left of my hair falls in curls around my neck. As I'm talking, Charlie makes a face and whispers, "Watch out."

Coming towards us are Pearl, Kat, Holly and Lauren. They're all wearing butt-hugging denim cutoffs, tights and a skimpy tank with THE PINK LADIES stenciled across it. Their hair is BIG and their makeup is HEAVY. Think bright pink lips and false eyelashes that defy gravity. Suddenly, I'm relieved I was the wrong shape for The Pink Ladies.

They stop in front of us and I wait for the inevitable comment about how I look. But no one says anything. In fact, they aren't even looking at me, but are staring—perfect pink mouths hanging open with disgust—at Betty, Charlie and Amber.

I've been so wrapped up in myself I haven't really looked at them. Like The Pink Ladies, they're wearing tanks, but theirs have THE PANTY LINERS printed across in swirling Gothic script. Also, they're in seventies-style polyester running shorts, but they aren't showing perfect stomachs. Instead, they're revealing enormous hip-hugger granny panties that they've pulled up and tucked into their tops.

The girls stare at each other.

"What do *you* look like?" asks Pearl.

"You," replies Betty, laughing. Well, Pearl fed her that line. And it really is funny. The Panty Liners look like a warped mirror image of The Pink Ladies. I suppose it's the worst thing in the world to do, but I can't help myself. I laugh, loudly. Quickly, I clap my hand over my mouth.

Pearl twists round and does a double take, her fake lashes batting wildly. "It's *you*!" she says. There is silence. Pearl, for once in her life, is lost for words. Then she gets a grip, sucks in a sharp breath like a snake preparing to strike, and opens her mouth. I tense, but her furious face melts into a huge smile.

"Hi, Ollie," she says, standing a little taller. He has appeared by my side. "We were all admiring *her* new look." She nods in my direction. Ollie looks at me, and I mean properly looks at me, from my toes to my hair, and he smiles, but he doesn't say anything. I feel myself blushing and fight the temptation to shrink back behind Betty.

"My sister did it," he says. Now Pearl can't say a thing.

"Let's go, girls," she finally manages. "We're actually

farther up the line, Ollie. Come and find us." As they leave, she gives him her sweetest smile. Kat glances back at me over her shoulder.

The line starts to shuffle forward and eventually Ollie and I are handed a number and sent into a large room with black walls. The Panty Liners disappear through another door. In the gloom, I immediately notice The Pink Ladies. Sitting on the floor along with the other dancers, they seem less intimidating, smaller even.

When Pearl isn't looking, Kat manages to smile at me and mouth, "Love it!" tugging quickly at her hair. I'm about to turn away when out of nowhere she shoots her "Sniffin' Jake" face at me. I can't help smiling, loving and hating her at the same time. Ollie's been a powerful distraction over the past week, but seeing Kat with Pearl hurts. I know I should give up on her and admit she's a bad friend . . . but I miss her so much.

"Listen up!" A young man, dressed in a slim-fitting black shirt and dark jeans, is standing in the stage area, a large space marked out with white tape. "I'm Nathan, a producer on *Starwars*, and I'll be one of your judges tonight, along with Tania over there." He gestures to an older woman with dark, swinging hair who is standing in the shadows. "You've all got a number and will be called up in order. You get five minutes, maybe less—it depends if we like you. Don't worry, we can tell who's got potential in that time, so no hysterics if we stop your music and ask you to leave." He pauses to allow his words to sink in. "Good luck, everyone. Group one . . . Rhapsody? You're up first."

We are group seventeen.

A group of girls stumble to their feet, hand over their music, then get into position. They dance for less than two minutes before Nathan shouts out, "Thank you! Exit to the left, please. Group two, up you come." It's so quick. I can't believe all our hard work could be over in a matter of minutes.

Group two is actually a boy dancing alone to Michael Jackson's "Thriller." He's good and funny, and he dances with such confidence. When he finishes—he's allowed to do his whole dance—we get to clap. Nathan and Tania confer for a moment.

"Thank you!" calls out Nathan. "Take a seat."

So that's how it works. If you're through, you sit down, but if they don't want you, you leave immediately.

They fly through the dances and it isn't long before The Pink Ladies, group fourteen, are up. I actually feel nervous for them. As Betty predicted, they're using an R&B track, but their dance isn't just bump and grind. They begin by barely moving, just shrugging their shoulders, then they introduce a new move every few seconds. It is tight, well rehearsed and subtle. In some ways, it reminds me of a show dance, like *Chicago*, but much faster.

They get a huge round of applause and I'm not surprised when they're told to sit down. Pearl is grinning, but not in the mean little way she normally smiles; instead, her whole face is beaming. I'm taken back to junior school and the last time I saw *that* smile. I vividly remember swinging Pearl round on the end of my sweater—she was grinning up at me—then I let her go and sent her flying across the field. Mum told me off for stretching the arms. Then, as though Pearl can read my thoughts in the darkness of the room, the mask falls back into place and her smile vanishes.

Soon, group sixteen is performing. Only three groups have been told to stay behind so far. I jump when Ollie leans across to me and whispers, "You can do the knickerbocker."

"What do you mean?"

"Tonight, in a minute. I'm going to lead you into the move. You can do it!"

"No way. Seriously, Ollie. That's crazy, we can't even—" But I don't get the chance to finish.

"Thank you, group sixteen," says Nathan, pushing his thick-rimmed glasses up his nose. "Clearly going for the sympathy vote. Exit on the left, please. Group seventeen, up you come!" Ollie jumps to his feet and I follow, telling myself over and over to relax, smile and put my shoulders back. I must look like an evil goblin as I run to the front, desperately twisting my mouth into a casual smile.

Having sorted out the music, Ollie joins me at the center of the stage, puts his arm around me and we stand in the close hold. Lulu decided that we should start almost as though we are frozen in the middle of the dance. The room around us falls silent. We look at each other, then move closer together. Our bodies lock and I can feel our hearts beating. Then our music kicks in and I feel the familiar surge that I always get when I hear the opening drums . . . two more beats and we're off!

I know we're dancing well. We're quicker than ever and totally in tune with each other. I can feel our confidence, and, I guess, so can the audience. Ollie is focused and every one of our turns and spins is tight, fast and smooth. As we come to the end of our dance, we haven't missed a step.

Ollie swings me to face him. This isn't in our routine!

He looks at me, raises his eyebrows as a warning, then pushes me away. I have no choice but to go for it. If I don't, our dance will end with us in a heap on the floor. Ollie pulls me back across his arm and his hand catches me on my lower back, pushing my legs up. I try to flip over as Ollie lifts me higher and higher. The room rushes past, but not fast enough. I can't make it! If I stop midair, Ollie will drop me. In a panic, I squeeze his shoulder desperately trying to communicate this. Then I'm falling back the way I've come, landing heavily on my feet. I stumble back, but Ollie whips me up and spins me twice to finish the dance.

The music stops and the room is silent. My cheeks burn. I couldn't do it. I ruined the dance. But, also, I'm angry. Ollie and I weren't partners then—he was doing *his* dance, and I got in the way. His fingers loosen away from mine and our hands fall apart.

Then there is a clap, followed by another and another and another. We look at the judges because it doesn't matter what everyone else thinks—they will decide if we get through. The applause dies away. They talk for a second and Nathan makes some notes. "Thank you," he says, frowning slightly. He hesitates for a second, then gives us a nod. "Sit down. Group eighteen."

Relief floods through my body and my heart pounds as we stumble through the remaining dancers.

"Why did you do that?" I whisper as soon as we're sitting down. "I looked like an idiot!"

"Don't talk about it, please. It was stupid." He's staring at the floor. Then he looks up with a look of amazement on his face. "But, we did it, Bea. Can you believe it?"

"Not really." I shake my head. I desperately want to

talk to him about everything—about our dance, his little "surprise" and how I murdered the knickerbocker, but I have to wait. Pearl leans over to Ollie and soon their heads are together and she's whispering and smiling.

Are they talking about me? I turn away. This is me being fierce. I'm not going to let Pearl, or my stupid, hopeless shoulder-love for Ollie ruin the fact that we have got through the auditions. Ollie and *me*. We did it together.

"Watch *Starwars* on Saturday," says Nathan when all the groups have auditioned and there is a handful of us left in the black room. "It's footage from the auditions all over the country and you may spot yourselves. The next episodes will show each round of the semifinals and then the finals will be live."

We walk out of the Brighton Centre together and I get a text from Betty saying they left over an hour ago. Pearl puts up with me because of Ollie, and I listen while she goes over every detail of their dance. I may be walking with Ollie and Kat as well, but just being near Pearl makes me slip quietly into the background.

When we get to the seafront, they turn towards town, but Ollie hangs back. "Are you coming with us to KFC?" he asks. Pearl rolls her eyes. "You can get the train back with us."

I can't let Ollie see me like this, a shadow of myself. "Thanks," I say. "But I'll head out now."

"Come on. Big Daddy? Boneless Banquet?" he says. "Don't be scared . . . They're nicer than they sound."

"I can't. See you tomorrow?" He looks slightly baffled, but he shrugs and follows Pearl. Kat goes too, having given me the tiniest of Ladybird waves. I stand alone on the pavement. Mum wouldn't have cared if I'd got back an hour late, but what can I do? My eyes sting as all the magic of the evening falls away from me and I see Pearl slip her arm through Ollie's. A sick feeling stirs my stomach. That's *my* arm she's touching and *my* shoulder she's resting her head against.

How hopeless: short, quiet, round Bea versus spectacular, glittering Pearl. As I walk towards the station, pink streetlights blink on, one after another, and the storm clouds hide the last glimpses of blue.

7.

In tutor time, Betty's wearing her "Panty Liners" tank top and, for some reason, a pair of Peppa Pig sunglasses. "Can you believe it, Bea? We didn't get through!"

"Take it all off, Betty," says Mr. Simms.

She does, but accidentally-on-purpose gets the tank top stuck on her head where she leaves it piled up like a turban. "How about you and Ollie?" she says. "The weird situation has just got a whole lot weirder! You are going to be on TV dancing 'jive' with Ollie *McFittie* Matthews. Weird." She notices my anxious face. "But definitely *good* weird."

Is there such a thing as good weird? I suppose there is, I realize, as I watch Betty take a sip of hot tea from a mug she has hidden behind her bag. The mug has "Teaching Legend" printed below Mr. Simms's face. "Cookie?" she asks, pushing a packet of Sandies towards me.

I take a broken half and look around for Pearl. She's not here yet. Perhaps she'll give up her whole "destroy Bea" thing now she's seen Ollie abandon me on the streets of Brighton. Clearly, I'm not a threat.

But in French it turns out that I am.

Pearl and Lauren have gotten to the lesson early and when I go in they're flirting with Mr. Tweed at the front of the room. Lauren's writing on the whiteboard, stuff like "*Oui* ♥ French" and "*Mr. Tweed est la bombe!*" to distract him from Pearl's "art."

Now, although I hate to admit it, Pearl is good at drawing, which is why what she's doing is so effective. She's drawing a pig wearing roll-up jeans and a little cardigan. Next, she carefully adds short curly hair and a daisy clip, asking Mr. Tweed for a red pen to give the pig red lipstick, red nails and red shoes. The pig has a stomach rolling out over the top of its jeans. The pig is me. Everyone who walks in the room either knows this straightaway or gets told—that's Holly's job.

Kat's sitting in the front row, twisting her hair round and round her fingers. It's what she does when she's worried, but she doesn't get up and stop Pearl, and she doesn't look over at me.

Betty wanders in, looks at the picture and gives me a questioning look. I shrug. What can I do? If I put my hand up and say, "Mr. Tweed that big fat pig Pearl is drawing is supposed to be me," it will confirm what everyone suspects.

Plus, surely he'll wipe it off when the lesson starts?

Nope. We're watching a film about French markets, then working from textbooks so I have to look at it for the whole lesson. Before we leave the room, Betty asks if she can clean the white board. Mr. Tweed lets her, finally glancing up at what has been staring his class in the face for the past hour. He smiles appreciatively at Pearl's drawing skills.

"You've got to say or do *something*," says Betty, catching up with me outside the room. "The second you saw that picture you should have gone up to the front and just wiped it off. Or, even better, drawn a picture of her as Mr. Poo Head . . . with a big poo on her head . . . and a speech bubble saying, 'I'm Pearl and I'm a poo'—that would have been funny—anything would be better than just sitting there and taking it."

"I don't want to make things worse."

"But you're *not* doing anything and things *are* getting worse. You, Bea Hogg, need to grow some balls. Big ones!" Now this makes me laugh. In fact, I'm laughing so much I don't notice Ollie come up to us.

"Hey," he says, looking bemused. "My mum's away

this weekend so I'm having a party at my place on Saturday." He pauses for a second, before adding, "Tell Amber and Charlie. See you both there?" And he's gone again.

"Well," says Betty, "that was very *brief.* Ollie's not usually all shy like that."

"Do you think he was shy?"

"Yeah, definitely. Strange. Anyway, who cares . . . we're going to a party. We're going to a party!" she yells in a passing seventh grade boy's face. She manages to get a high five out of him.

"I don't know, Betty . . . Pearl will be there and she'll make me feel like—"

Betty cuts in, "No excuses, Bea. Where are your big balls? Come with the three of us and we'll never leave you alone for a second. How often do freshmen get invited to a sophomore's house party?"

"OK, OK." So that's it. I'm going to a party at Ollie's house. But what if he didn't really want to invite me, but had to because I was standing next to Betty? I must look worried because Betty grabs my arm and says, "Don't even think about trying to get out of this one. I want you around at my place at seven . . . no excuses."

"Little Bea Hogg!" says Betty's dad when I turn up. "I've missed you—you used to stay here at least once a week!"

"Is my toothbrush still in the bathroom?" I ask. It really is great to see him, a bit like coming home.

"Of course. There'll always be a toothbrush for you here." He ushers me in. "Follow the noise and you'll find Betty. She's going through a Juliette Gréco stage at the moment. Her mum would be so proud." As I go up the stairs, he calls after me, "Don't tell her I said that or she'll never listen to it again."

The jazz music leads me to her door, which is covered, and I mean *covered*, in lips cut out from magazines. I feel like I'm about to be eaten up. I push open the door and the throaty crooning French singer is suddenly drowned out by girly screaming.

"Bea! Get in and shut the door," says Betty. She is standing on her bed in her underwear pretending to smoke a breadstick. In a shocking French accent she announces that "tonight, we are going to be PROPER ladies, *Ladybirds* even," she adds with a wink to me, "doing zee makeup and zee giggling and all zat jazz!"

Two hours of makeup and frantic clothes-changing later, we walk to Ollie's. This takes a long time, because by now we are finding everything funny.

"Here we are, girls," says Betty as we turn down a road. "This is the home of *the* Ollie Matthews." I feel like there should be a blue plaque next to the door or a star shining above the roof, but it's just an ordinary semi like mine, perhaps with fewer Charlie and Lola stickers on the windows. All the lights are on and we can see it's packed because in each lit-up window there are moving shapes.

The door's been left open so we walk in. I recognize nearly everyone from school—it's mainly sophomores and juniors—but no one pays us any attention as we push our way through the crowded living room. Loud music makes talking impossible so we just follow Betty. She leads us to the kitchen. "Anyone care for a drink?" she asks, looking at what's on offer.

The worktop is awash with half-empty fizzy-drink bottles, along with a few beer cans and Bacardi Breezer bottles. We find some unopened cans of Coke in the fridge, but Betty zooms in on the alcohol and quickly makes herself a cocktail she calls "Brown" . . . because it's brown.

Going back through to the living room, we find space on the corner of a sofa to sit down. Well, there isn't room for all of us and I end up on the floor, but it's kind of nice just sitting there watching what's going on. We have a Bugles-eating competition, seeing how many we can fit in our mouths at once. Eventually, Charlie wins with fifteen, but then she gags and sprays them out over my hair so it doesn't count.

We're busy nominating someone to go and get more

snacks from the kitchen when Ollie sticks his head in the room and comes over. "If Mum comes back early from Blackpool, I'm dead," he tells us cheerfully. "I'm supposed to be at my sister's, but Lulu thinks I'm here watching a movie."

Suddenly, there's a crash as a girl who's started dancing flies into a plant on the windowsill. Ollie winces and looks slightly less relaxed.

"So, Ollie," says Betty, knocking back the dregs of her Brown, "you two jive beasts got through to the second round of *Starwars!*"

"We totally did, me and my Dancing Bean." He looks down at me and, despite the room that's heaving with bodies, my friends watching my every move and the heat and noise that surround us, I smile up at him and feel myself glowing. *My* Dancing Bean.

I want to pat the floor next to me and say, "Sit down," and then we can talk all evening, about everything . . . about how I broke my foot falling down a badger hole, how I can't click my fingers, how I stroked a baby penguin, about *everything*. I have a mad, fierce moment. I'm going to do it!

"Hey, Ollie," I say. "Why don't—" But before I can finish, Pearl pulls him round by the shoulder—where did she come from?—and slumps against him.

"There you are!" she says. "Come and dance with me." And she pulls him away from us, away from me, and into the middle of the room.

I shrink back into the corner and watch them do a sort of half-jive to the music. Pearl makes it look so easy and, as she moves around the room—and around Ollie—in her skinny jeans and loose top, everyone stops talking to watch them. It's amazing how the boys just can't take their eyes off her.

"Come on, Bea," said Betty, ruffling my curls. "Let's get another drink." And we head for the kitchen.

We hang out in there for a while, chatting to Charlie's brother, George, and his mates. I notice Lauren and Holly sitting in the garden, but there's no sign of Kat. By now Betty has moved on to "Orange" and she's laughing crazily at everything George says.

Pearl walks in, her cheeks glowing from dancing, and takes a long drink from a bottle that's handed to her. Sitting on the edge of the table, she fixes her large blue eyes on me.

"Bean," she says. "Do you like boys?" Around us, a few people stop talking. "Go on, you can tell me!" She laughs and throws back her head so that her wild hair trails down her back.

"Come on," I say to the others. "Let's go." But they don't hear me over the noise of the party.

"Ah, don't go, Jelly Bean . . . it's just a question." I need to get out of this kitchen, but Pearl is still staring at me, still smiling. I go to walk past her, but she lifts her legs up onto the work surface, trapping me. I turn to go the other way, but there are too many people. Behind me, Betty is attempting to make another Orange while Charlie and Amber try to stop her.

I'm alone.

"Answer the question," says Pearl, quietly. "Do you like boys? Yes or no?"

"Yes," I say, finally giving in to her. I want to go home now. The evening is ruined.

"Yeah, right," laughs Pearl. She still won't let me pass. Behind her, I see Ollie come into the kitchen. He stops and looks over at us. Most of the people around us have fallen silent, waiting to see what will happen.

"What's going on?"

"I was just asking if Bea was having fun," she says. "Wasn't I?" Ollie looks from Pearl to me.

"That's right," I say, trying to make my voice sound as normal as possible. Her legs drop down and she even gives my shoulder a stroke as I walk past. The girls follow me back to our corner in the living room.

A few minutes later, Pearl comes in the room holding hands with Ollie. She leads him into the hallway and up the stairs. I feel embarrassed and stupid, like I'm a million miles away from being the sort of person Ollie would want to be with.

"I'm going to call home for a ride," I say. They try to stop me, but I've made up my mind.

As I wait outside for Mum, the sounds of the party bubbling away behind me, I feel an ache growing inside my stomach. I glance at the upstairs windows. All the curtains are closed and I can't see a thing. I wonder if I ate too many Bugles?

No. I don't think so. I'm just totally and utterly jealous.

8.

I wake up to the sound of cartoons and the delicious smell of bacon cooking. Mum and Nan are chatting in the kitchen and the kettle's boiling. I roll over into a patch of sun shining in through the window and the airbed makes its wheezy noise. I start to doze off again, loving having my room to myself.

Suddenly, I hear a frantic patter of footsteps coming up the stairs and then along the hallway. Next, the door is thrown open.

"BEA!" Emma screams, launching herself across the room and landing on top of me. She puts her mouth to my ear and breathes there for a few seconds. I'm pinned beneath her, my mouth squashed into the pillow. "Guess what?" she says.

I can't reply. I can't even breathe.

"There's a WOMBLE in the garden!" Then she jumps off me and disappears as quickly as she arrived.

Now that's worth getting up to see.

For lunch, Nan makes one of her famous lasagnas and I have an enormous helping . . . with baked beans . . . and then Sara Lee cheesecake. Emma and I made the cheese-cake and it's good, even with her last minute Lego "decorations."

Nan smiles as I lick toffee off an angry-looking builder. "You're blooming, Bea. Just look at your rosy cheeks." She passes me the plate so I can have a second helping. "That'll be the jive. It's such a happy dance."

After lunch, I'm in such a blooming good mood that I agree to play "Trampabba" with Emma. It's a game she usually plays with Dad, but he's been away for so long she's starved of fun.

Mum puts the CD player on the kitchen windowsill and blares out "Dancing Queen." We don't need to worry about upsetting the neighbors as our house is at the end of the row and Mr. and Mrs. Pilkington, who live next door, happen to be slightly deaf Abba fans.

Next, Emma and I get up onto the trampoline and bounce and dance like three-year-olds. I hold Emma's sticky little hands and jump as high as I can, and I realize that I can keep going much longer than I usually can. I'm getting thighs of steel!

"Dancinween! Dancinween!" Emma shrieks from somewhere around my knees.

In fact, she's shrieking so loudly that I don't hear the doorbell ring, my mum calling out to me, or someone coming into the garden. It's only when Emma cries out, "It's Holly!" that I realize we have company.

It's not Holly—Pearl would never allow that—it's Ollie. He grins and wanders over to us. I immediately stop jumping, but Emma and I have built up a lot of momentum and it's difficult to look casual on a trampoline with an overexcited toddler bouncing around your ankles . . . when you're wearing a wig. Did I mention the wig?

Mum turns off the CD player and calls Emma in to watch *Postman Pat*. Well, she doesn't like that and makes her feelings clear by climbing up me like a monkey and clinging onto my head.

"Bounce with Holly!" she screams from somewhere inside my wig. Mum peels her off me, finally getting her inside with the bribe of "getting two hamsters."

Suddenly, the garden is very quiet. "We were playing Trampabba," I say, still bouncing a bit.

Ollie nods as though he fully understands and then sits on the edge of the trampoline. He looks up at me. "I thought maybe we could have an extra practice. Lulu gave me the keys to the hall and they haven't got lessons until five."

"OK. I can do that," I say, and then I have a flash of fierce inspiration, "But there is one condition."

"What?"

"You must warm up with a quick round of Trampabba."

"Agreed," he says, seriously, putting his hand out to me. I pull him up. "Where's my wig?"

I hand him Emma's discarded afro. Out of the corner of my eye, I see Mum and Nan peering out of the kitchen window and then my nan's hand reaching out to press "play" on the CD player. "Take a Chance on Me" fills the garden.

She *so* chose that song. "Shall we?" I ask.

"Let's," Ollie replies, taking both of my hands, just like I did with Emma, and starting to bounce. We start small, but soon there's no stopping us. You go much higher with a fifteen-year-old than a three-year-old. "I didn't see you leave last night," he yells over to me.

"You weren't around," I reply.

"Right," he says. "Sorry about that. You should have stayed." I do a rather impressive "butt jump" and land back up on my feet. Inspired, Ollie, gets up a bit of height, then shouts, "Watch out: I'm going to do a knickerbocker!"

9.

Over the next week, we rehearse later and later as we perfect our routine and wait for the *Starwars* auditions to be shown on TV. School has become a complicated game of Pearl avoidance and each afternoon, when I step into the dance studio, I feel my shoulders relaxing.

At the end of Friday's rehearsal, Ollie hands me an envelope. "There are tickets in there so your family can come and watch us being filmed," he says. "They want shots of our adoring fans."

We're standing by the exit to the hall. I wait for him to suggest we meet up for an extra practice or watch *Starwars* together on Saturday night, or something else amazing like that, but he doesn't say anything. He must have plans and I know who they involve. He pauses. The envelope slips out of my hand and lands by his left foot. We both bend down to pick it up, but I get there first and bump his chin with my forehead on the way up.

"Oops, clumsy head!" I say.

"Right," he says, grabbing his bag, "I'd better go." He opens the door and looks at me for a moment longer, rubbing his chin. His eyes make me do a thousand internal knickerbockers.

"See you," I say, but the door has slammed shut behind him. Clumsy head. Clumsy head?

The next day, Emma's allowed to stay up late to see "Bea's film!" (she is going to be *so* disappointed) and the Silver Stitchers start arriving from 5:00 p.m. We all squeeze into the living room and I'm given the best spot in the middle of the sofa. On the coffee table, Nan and the Stitchers have arranged a "you're on TV" feast: There are egg salad sandwiches, bowls and bowls of chips, cups of tea rattling on every surface along with tall glasses of "fizz" squeezed into the gaps.

Right in the middle of it all is a cake, made by Marion that she's decorated to look like my face. She's done my hair with licorice pinwheels (strangely accurate) and used Tic Tacs for my teeth (strangely chilling). Underneath my face, she's piped "Bea Rocks" in wobbly icing. It's fair to say she's better at sewing than sugarcraft.

"You should have asked Betty and Kat round," says Mum as she nestles in next to me on the sofa. Honestly, mothers don't understand a thing. Kat and I hardly talk these days and Betty has probably arranged a rave with a gang of friends and a vat of Orange. I wonder what Kat's doing tonight, if she's watching *Starwars* with Pearl. For a moment, I think about texting her, but then I'd be admitting I still want us to be friends.

"Quiet!" screams Nan, sloshing her sparkling wine on Emma's head. A trailer for *Starwars* has just come on. There's heavy military music, close-ups of tear-streaked faces and then the screen goes black before STARWARS: LET THE BATTLE COMMENCE is spelled out in a shower of stars. The Silver Stitchers scream and I hide behind a cushion. Marion rushes into the kitchen to put another bottle of bubbly in the fridge.

When she gets back, the ads are coming to an end and I'm still hiding behind my cushion. Suddenly, the opening credits appear. Stars swirl around a black sky and then, to thudding music, the word *Starwars* appears, at first tiny but gradually getting bigger and bigger until it fills the screen.

"Oh, Bea," squeals Mum. "I'm so excited!"

"Where's Bea?" asks Emma. "That Bea?" She points at

the presenter, Shad Montague, a six-foot, suntanned, ex–reality-TV star, wearing a dinner jacket and bow tie. "Oh. That a man. Not Bea."

"Shush," I say.

"Welcome to *Starwars: Battle of the Dancers!*" says Shad, twinkling at the camera. "We've been searching every corner of Great Britain to find the very best young dancers our country has to offer. Of course, we also had to let a lot of people go because, well, they weren't quite *battle ready* as you can see for yourselves . . ."

"Shad has got beautiful buns!" gasps Jean, our oldest Stitcher. She tends to say whatever pops into her head. The next twenty-five minutes are taken up with footage of the dancers who didn't get through and interviews with them afterwards.

"That Bea?" asks Emma every time a new face appears on the screen, while Jean offers her expert opinion on every dancer. We get "strange ears," "looks like a tart" and "moves like Marion after she's eaten peas."

Finally, in the last five minutes, successful dancers are shown. I recognize a couple of faces and then see the Michael Jackson wannabe. "He was with my group!" I yell, pointing at the screen.

Shad's commentary starts up again, "Luckily for Jake, our judges were blown away with his Wacko moves. Same goes for Ollie and Bea, who've rock 'n' rolled their way to the semifinals!" And there we are, for around seven seconds, spinning around the stage.

"That Bea?" asks Emma.

"Yes!" we all cry. And then we are gone from the screen only to be replaced with a couple of seconds of The Pink Ladies.

"Beatrice, you looked absolutely stunning!" says Nan, wide-eyed. Mum just clutches me to her and wipes a tear from her eye. "What you learnt in just a week is incredible," Nan adds. "I can't wait to see you at the semis. Can we come and watch it being filmed?" There's a ripple of excitement in the room and all the Stitchers' eyes light up.

I've been dreading this moment. I'm going to be stressed out enough in London without worrying about Nan and what she'll be saying . . . or doing . . . or wearing. Will it be her Topshop tassel dress (lime green) or her Miss Selfridge pantsuit (strapless)? Will the Stitchers make a banner and will Marion be responsible for sewing my face?

"I don't know," I say. "It's next Wednesday so Mum's working and you'll be looking after Emma."

"I could change my shift. We could all come!" Mum looks really excited, but I'm not. I can just imagine them having to stop filming because Emma won't stop shouting out, "That Bea? That Holly?" every five seconds, and the idea of Pearl being close to the people I love, laughing at them . . . I couldn't stand it.

"Don't worry about it," I say. "It'll get complicated. I'd rather just go up with Lulu."

There are a few moments of silence.

"Whatever you want, love," says Nan, giving me a big squishy hug. "We'll be able to watch you on TV." I bury my face in Nan's shoulder and try to ignore Mum's hurt look, and the waves of disappointment coming from the Silver Stitchers.

10.

On the train up to London, Ollie and I sit in silence, staring out of different windows. We've practiced till we're ready to drop, but although our routine is fast and slick, we still can't do the knickerbocker. I don't think I'm capable of talking, so I focus on watching cows flash past. Lulu does her best, but in the end she just gives up and flicks through a magazine.

We go on the underground to get to the TV studios and then it's a five-minute walk. Even though we're just a couple of hours from home, London is a different world. There's a stream of people all walking in the direction of the studio and we fall in step with them. Most are wearing security tags around their necks and everything about the way they move and dress says, "We belong here."

The studio is a huge, curving white building and we have to go through security just to get into the lobby. Uniformed guards check our bags and even pat us down. Next, we line up at the desk with the *Starwars* sign hanging over it. There are a few serious-faced girls waiting ahead of us with their mums. They have elaborate hair and makeup as though they are about to step onstage.

Ollie and I glance at each other. We are *totally* out of our element.

"Don't worry, my darlings," says Lulu, putting her arms around us. "If you manage to get through the semis, we have three *whole* weeks. You can learn some Lindy Hop—it looks amazing—and we'll crack the aerials so you'll have something incredible for the finals."

"*If* we get through," says Ollie.

"*It don't mean a thing, if you ain't got that swing,*" sings Lulu softly.

"What's that?" I ask.

"Duke Ellington, a swing classic. You two have *swing*. You have *jive*, the best dance in the world. That's why you *will* get through. It's what I repeat to myself before I compete."

"Hey, I've got something like that," I say, but I trail off when the lobby doors swing open and Pearl comes straight up to Ollie and throws her arms round his neck. The Pink Ladies fall in behind her. Lulu rolls her eyes. This makes me feel better.

"I'm sooo nervous!" cries Pearl, standing close, her hands resting on Ollie's shoulders.

I risk a smile at Kat, and she makes her eyes go big and round, like an owl. I realize that this is all she can risk, this is her smile . . . it's better than nothing. I do the same face back at her and she slams her hand over her mouth, trying not to laugh.

By now, we're at the front of the line and Lulu pulls Ollie over to sort out all the forms. They seem to be having an argument.

"Bea," says Ollie, "what's your favorite animal?"

"Monkeys," I reply without hesitating.

"Exactly. Me too!"

Soon, we're led along a complicated series of corridors by a girl named Gem. She has a wave of thick blond hair that falls over one eye and she's wearing an oversized tank top with DIE FACEBOOK DIE printed across it. She out-cools even Pearl. After going in the elevator, down two sets of stairs and across a courtyard, we stand outside a set of double doors that are big enough to drive a bus through. "Welcome to studio six, the *Starwars* studio," says Gem, pulling open one of the doors.

We stream in and there is a collective gasp. The stage is vast and stretches into the rows of seating. The black backdrop towers behind the stage and it's spangled with LED stars. It's like gazing into the night sky.

Once the doors shut behind us, there's no natural light, just powerful spotlights that swing across the auditorium. The lighting crew must be experimenting because the lights keep changing color. I look at Ollie and watch his face go green, then magenta. Pearl is whispering in his ear and pointing at another group of girls. A blue light sweeps across them both.

Gem waves in the direction of the seats that rise all around us. "These will be full in a few hours," she says casually. The talking dies away.

Telling the adults to take a seat, she leads the dancers up a flight of backlit glass stairs to the main stage. We stand and look out. It's impossible to spot Lulu because the lights are so bright. It's hot too. The girls who are already made up have sweat trickling down their faces. Gem notices too. "Sorry, guys, I'm afraid we're going to have to redo your makeup," she says. "It has to be special for TV. In fact, that's where I'm going to take you now."

The boys are separated from the girls and we spend the next hour and a half getting ready. It's carefully organized and the makeup artists have little cards of information on each of us where they've planned our look in advance. I'm given the full fifties treatment, and it's much more dramatic than Lulu's makeover.

"Gorgeous skin," says Harry, my makeup artist. "And, my goodness, these are whoppers!" I look up quickly, but he's gazing into my eyes as he carefully applies individual false eyelashes. "Beautiful gray peepers," he says, smiling down at me.

Harry moves on to my hair and, if such a thing is possible, makes it even bigger. "I love it!" he cries, burying his hands in my curls. "I could curl up and die in there!" Pearl, who's sitting a few seats away from me, chats away to her makeup artist asking for more of this and less of that. Harry outlines my lips with a scarlet pencil and then uses a little brush to fill them in with a fire-truck-red lipstick. "Oh my God," he says, standing back to admire the effect. "These smackers should come with a health warning!"

I smile at Harry in the mirror and try to think of something to say, something that will let him know how much I love the kind things he's saying to me . . . but I feel too shy.

"Thank you," is all I can whisper when I look, amazed, at the final, glamorous fifties film-star version of me.

"You're welcome, honey," he says, squeezing my shoulders.

Our "changing room" looks like a conference room, but the curtains are shut and mirrors have been arranged everywhere. All around me, girls strip to their undies and start parading up and down the room, competing to be the most laid-back. The Pink Ladies are hidden away in the other corner of the room and I'm all on my own.

A beautiful Scottish girl with cropped hair thrusts a mirror in my hand and says, "Hold this a sec." Then she pulls out a pair of tweezers, pulls down her leggings and starts to perfect her bikini line. *How have I come to be here?*

When she takes back the mirror, I slip on new jeans, rolled up and tight round my ankles, and another of Lulu's tops. It's a black shirt with a red collar and buttons. Following Lulu's strict instructions, I knot it at the waist. Before I go to find Ollie, I glance in the mirror.

I stop and stare, peering a bit closer. I look brighter, taller, more colorful . . . I'm blooming! I fight the urge to smile at my reflection. "Hello, Bea," I want to say. "There you are!" I tear myself away, realizing I must find Ollie before we miss our rehearsal slot on the stage.

He's waiting in the corridor. "Wow!" he says, his eyes going wide. Does he mean, wow—amazingly beautiful, or, wow—freaky clown face? *Really* hard to tell. In case it's freaky clown face, I quickly turn and walk in what seems like the right direction.

"Come on," I call over my shoulder. "We'll be late."

After we've rehearsed, we're shown into another large room where we wait until filming starts. There's a table covered with sandwiches, bottles of water, granola bars and chocolate brownies and a tower of beautifully arranged fruit. Usually, I'd have piled up a plate but, like everyone else in the room, I have no appetite.

The first group called up, Bo Salsa, is a couple doing a Latin dance to fast guitar music, the next a group of street dancers. As each group comes back, sweating and grinning with relief, they're cheered back in. I love the atmosphere and if I wasn't so nervous—and if Pearl wasn't hanging around Ollie—I might be able to enjoy myself. Gem comes back in with her clipboard. "Jive Monkey, you're next."

"Come on," said Ollie. "This is it!"

"What?"

"That's us: Jive Monkey. Lulu wanted Jive Bunny, but I told her no way. I said we'd keep the 'Jive' but we needed to be a cooler animal."

"Jive *Monkey*?"

"Don't look like that. You chose it. You said it was your favorite."

"Come on, you two," snaps Gem impatiently and we get moving.

"Good luck, babe!" calls Pearl.

I guess she's talking to Ollie.

We stand backstage while House Party, a girl group, performs. We can hear their music and the audience's crazy reaction to them, but we can't see anything. I know Ollie's family are watching and now I wish I had one person out there who would be yelling just for me . . . even if that one person was sixty-five and wearing a tight satin playsuit.

The audience goes wild as House Party's track fades out.

I take a deep breath and look at Ollie. We attempt a smile and fail. Instead we hold hands. It's just how we go onstage. "Bea?" he whispers.

"Yeah?"

"What's the thing you say?"

"What thing?"

"Like Lulu's 'It don't mean a thing . . .' "

The applause is petering out and Shad talks into the microphone.

"It's Shakespeare," I say. "Something Nan taught me—"

"Tell me."

" 'Though she be but little, she is fierce.' "

Gem pops out of the shadows and whispers, "On in five." Listening to her earpiece, pulling it close so she can hear over the applause, she holds up her hands and starts to take away her fingers, counting us down. "Four, three, two," she mouths—House Party sweeps past us—"one!"

Together we leave the gloom of backstage and emerge into dazzling lights, swinging into a perfect close hold in the center of the stage. Blackness and stars surround us. The audience is silent, waiting. Our eyes lock, something we've rehearsed, and Ollie says, quietly, but perfectly clear, "Be fierce, Bea."

I nod, our track kicks in, and we hit our first move with perfect timing. I don't think or worry, I just dance, and I know from our first steps, that we're fast and sharp, better than ever. We are filled with energy and something is different. Perhaps it's the heat of the lights, or the cries of the audience, or maybe it's the baseline of our track, which is so loud I can feel the vibrations in my body.

Ollie spins me, dips me, slows it down, speeds it up. And we keep the eye contact—something Lulu has been trying to get us to do for days—and smile at the same time and laugh at the same time. Our feet move faster, our hands fall together firmly and before I know it, we're dancing our final steps. Ollie swings me away and, backwards, I drop back into his hands so he can push me into a lift. It's not a full aerial, but it still looks good.

The studio erupts with applause before my feet have returned to the ground. We stand there catching our breath and laughing. Shad runs up to join us and stands between us, arms round our heaving shoulders. "How about that? How much do we love Jive Monkey?" Obediently, the audience yell back, giving him what he wants. "So, Ollie, do you think you've got what it takes to win *Starwars*?"

"Well, we've got a few surprises for the final," he says, without missing a beat, "so we hope we get to show you just what we're capable of."

Shad turns to me. "Bea, what brought you two together to form Jive Monkey?"

I say the first thing that comes into my head, "My nan made me." There's a moment's silence and then the audience laughs and I wish Nan was sitting in the audience, nudging the people next to her to let them know who she is.

"So, you two, *jive*? Bit of a grannies' dance, isn't it?"

"Not if you do it fast enough," says Ollie.

"Well, I just hope the judges want to see your next dance as much as we do. Let's hear it again for Jive Monkey!"

As we exit, The Pink Ladies rush past us.

Ollie's shoulder brushes Pearl's arm, but she's so focused she doesn't even notice.

When we've all performed, we line up onstage while the judges' decision is announced. There are several cameras panning up and down the row, filming our anxious faces.

We stand in silence while Shad prepares the audience. Intense white lights shine in our eyes and I can't see beyond Shad. Ollie doesn't hold my hand. He stares at the ground.

"Only five of these amazing dance acts can go through to the *Starwars* final," Shad says, before pausing for several painful seconds. "In a few moments, there are going to be some broken dreams on this stage because I have in my hand the judges' decision." He holds a stiff gold envelope towards a camera and then turns to us. "When I open this, you will know if you are on your way to the finals or going home for good."

He turns back to face the audience and a drum roll begins, growing with intensity until my heart shakes with each crash. "If I call your name, you are through." Abruptly, the drums stop and he pulls open the envelope.

"The judges loved the sophisticated, contemporary shine of this all-girl act. Congratulations to . . . The Pink Ladies! You are through to the finals!"

I am shocked and disappointed. I am a horrible person. I'd almost forgotten they were competing with us. It's unusual enough having two groups from the same school in the semis—no way will we both get through to the finals. Cheering rings through the studio and there's a flurry of movement and screaming as the girls rush forward to the front of the stage.

Now I hang my head like Ollie. I can't believe we've come this far only for it to end right now, this minute. No more jive . . . no more close holds . . . no more—

Interrupting my thoughts, Shad reads the names of two more groups: Recall and Tribe. Mild hysteria ensues as the Recall boys start backflipping and the Tribe girls start crying. Meanwhile, I ache with disappointment.

Filming pauses for a moment as the semifinalists are reined back in. A girl with a slate steps in front of Shad and snaps it shut.

"You're a hot Latin act who got the judges' pulses racing . . ." Ollie and I visibly sag. "Bo Salsa! Boom! *You* could be starring in the West End!" I barely notice their reaction. I am never going to dance with Ollie again. I'm not losing a competition—I'm losing *me*. The *shyness* will sweep back and consume me.

"It's us." Ollie's shaking me. "He said Jive Monkey. We did it!" He pulls me forward, down the steps to the front of the stage. Shad gives me a big hug and I grin and grin.

"So, Bea, I take it you're surprised and happy!"

All I can do is smile and nod and the audience laughs. Shad has a more coherent conversation with Ollie while I grin towards the lights, wishing Mum and Nan were here watching me.

This time, as we travel home on the train, I get to discuss every second of the show with Ollie and Lulu. We grab a tray of Krispy Kreme doughnuts at the station and spend the journey eating all twelve and analyzing every move we made.

"I knew you had a chance when you ran on," says Lulu. "You were relaxed—amazing really—but more relaxed than I've ever seen you. Especially you, Bea."

"I was terrified," I say.

"No. You were *fierce*," says Ollie.

"Wait until you see yourself on TV," says Lulu.

I call Mum for the tenth time and leave a message on her phone. Why can't she pick up? No one's answering at home either and Nan's cell is switched off. I guess Mum's doing something disgusting involving blood and stitches, and Nan's got the TV turned up high.

The journey flies by and we're still laughing as we walk along the platform. At first, I don't notice Mum standing there behind the barrier.

"Bea," she calls, giving me a wave.

"Mum!" I run up to her and we hug. I feel so bad that I stopped her from coming up to London. "We got through! Can you believe it?"

"That's fantastic!" she says, but her voice sounds all wrong and then I notice her red eyes and how hard her mouth is trying to smile.

"What's wrong?"

"I'm sorry, Bea. It's Nan," she says. Her voice scares me.

"What's happened? Tell me."

"She's really sick, Bea. She's in the hospital." The station seems to disappear and my happiness drains from my body into the cold, chewing-gum-stained concrete floor. I feel sick. "They're doing everything they can to help her. She collapsed at home."

"Where's Emma?"

"At the Pilkingtons'."

"Is she alright?"

"I think she found it exciting," she says, "the ambulance and everything. Nan tried to make it seem like a game."

"But what's wrong?"

"She's had a stroke, Bea. And it's not looking good." I stare at Mum. She's holding my hands and trying not to cry, but I can't understand what she's saying. Thoughts about Nan fly through my head: her yellow hair, her tummy, her lasagna, the time I threw cards at her during a stressful game of gin rummy, how I wouldn't let her come and watch me today, even though I knew how desperately she wanted to . . . and how it's *not looking good*, and then I see what Mum is trying to tell me, what "not looking good" really means.

"It happened so quickly," she says, and then she starts

crying, so I do too and all my beautiful makeup that I'd left on to show Nan becomes a big smudgy mess on my face.

I have to tell Nan that I'm sorry about the playing cards and not letting her come to London. "Can I see her?" I ask.

"No. She's too sick, and at the moment she's having an operation. I've got to get back so that I'm there when she wakes up. Bea, I need to drop you at home so you can go and get Emma from next door. She'll be trying to ride Ralph. She's still convinced he's a horse." This makes us smile. "Can you look after her until I get back? It might be very late."

Mum and Lulu have a chat, and I look at Ollie who's standing off to one side. I almost laugh because he looks so worried and I look so grim, but then the almost-laugh threatens to become a big sob so I clamp my mouth shut and screw up my toes.

"Sorry, Bea," he says.

I nod, then follow Mum out of the station.

11.

Emma is very distracting.

We eat spaghetti hoops and cheese on toast, even though it's hours past her bedtime, and then watch all five episodes of her favorite *Postman Pat* DVD . . . twice. I hear the theme song twenty times. I try not to cry—because of Emma—but it's hard. I have a constant ache inside me. When Emma thinks I'm sad, she gives me another toy until there's hardly room for us on the sofa.

The phone rings all evening and I have to keep telling aunties, uncles and cousins what Mum has told me, which isn't much. Dad rings from deepest Mexico to tell me that there are no flights for forty-eight hours and that Mum should call him as soon as she comes back from the hospital. I tell him about *Starwars* and he puts a lot of effort into being excited for me. "Make sure you record every single second you're on TV," he says before he gets cut off with a huge crackle of static.

Eventually, Emma falls asleep on my lap. She has tomato sauce over her face and looks like a baby vampire. The phone rings again and I answer it straightaway so I don't wake her.

"Hello," I whisper.

"Hi, it's Ollie," says a voice that still manages to make me feel happy despite what is happening. "Why are you so quiet?"

"My sister's asleep on me."

"So . . . what're you doing?"

"Watching *Postman Pat*."

"But Emma's asleep."

"It's my favorite episode: 'Postman Pat and the Hole in the Road' . . . it's a really big hole."

"My mum made me a Postman Pat birthday cake once," says Ollie, "and put a photo of my face on it so I was sitting in the van between Pat and Jess."

"I can beat that. My nan once made me a birthday cake decorated with frozen peas."

"Why?"

"Because I asked for a Princess and the Pea cake, but without the princess," I say, "and because frozen peas taste good."

"Your nan's cool."

"I know." I hesitate, then decide to tell him something that's bothering me, even though it isn't as funny as frozen peas. "I don't think I realized that until today. Do you know, I wouldn't let her come up to London because I was embarrassed of her."

"You're embarrassed of everything, Bea: jive, Barbie, your red shoes . . ."

"How do you know that?" I ask.

"I'm very wise."

"Yeah, well, I'm not embarrassed of my red shoes anymore."

"Prove it."

"How?"

"Wear them to school."

"OK . . . and I'll dye my hair to match."

"Why not complete the look with a red nose."

I think for a moment. "I *do not* have clown hair!"

But now I'm laughing and my bouncing legs wake up Emma, who growls at me.

"I'd better go," I say.

"OK, see you tomorrow."

"Thanks for calling . . ."

"That's alright, bye . . ."

"See you . . ."

"Bye . . ."

"Yeah, bye . . ."

"OK, bye . . ."

"LOVE YOU!" screams Emma. I gasp and hang up. Emma looks furious. "I wanted to speak to Daddy."

"That wasn't Daddy, Emma."

I tuck her into bed and help her pretend to be a guinea pig—an essential part of her bedtime routine. She begins to doze off immediately. "Emma," I whisper.

"Uh?" she mutters.

"If you're talking to a boy on the phone and he doesn't want to hang up, does that mean he likes you?"

"Yes . . . no . . . ugh," she says.

"Thanks, Emma."

"Not Emma . . . guinea pig."

"Weee," I say, and turn off the light.

"Weee."

12. ♡

"Mmmm, nice shoes," says Pearl, the second I set foot in homeroom.

Suddenly, I feel really tired. After all, I only slept for a few hours last night. Mum crept into my room and woke me up at around 4:00 a.m. to tell me the operation had gone well and that Nan had "a chance." She said they would know more after Nan had a brain scan. It wasn't much, but I could sleep after that. I look down at my feet and see my red toes. I think about Nan on her own at the hospital. Then I feel angry.

I face Pearl. "Where did you get them? I want a pair," she continues, but with less enthusiasm than before. I don't say anything, but I don't look away either. "What are you staring at, freak?" she demands, pushing back her chair.

"I'm staring at *you*, Pearl," I say, and she walks towards me, her face confused and furious.

At that moment, Mr. Simms comes in, slurping at his cup of coffee. "Sit down, girls," he says, totally failing to notice the tension in the room, and we turn and walk away.

Betty raises her eyebrows at me and mouths, "Wow!"

I shrug at her. I just don't care what happens today. My fear for myself is tiny compared to my fear for Nan.

After school, we rehearse as usual and I insist that I feel fine: I know that dancing is the best distraction for me. "I've choreographed a whole new routine for you." Lulu speaks firmly. She is taking this seriously. "You've got just over two weeks and I want to make them count. First we'll demonstrate, and then I'll lead you through it. I've included several aerials and some Lindy hop."

"Lindy what?" asks Ollie.

"*Hop*. It's a jazz dance from the 1920s, very cool. It will surprise everyone. It has synchronized solo dancing and it looks amazingly laid-back." Ollie and I must look baffled, because Lulu says, "Just watch and learn. Now, you're going to see a lot of aerials. We won't start rehearsing them yet, but I know that you are really close to being able to do them. Trust me."

The music starts and they swing out of the close hold and almost straight into an aerial move. "That's the chuck!" yells Lulu as she flies, upside down, over Ray's shoulder, before landing with a delicate bounce and swinging back into the close hold.

"We are so dead," says Ollie under his breath.

"You're not dead," I say as, once again, Lulu is turned upside down, but this time as Ray swings her behind his back. "I am."

"Judo flip," Lulu calls out as Ray throws her up again.

"Yep. You're dead," agrees Ollie. The dance is incredible: fast, funny and, because of the crazy aerial moves, impressive. "And you expect us to do that?" asks Ollie the moment the music stops.

"You can, and you will," says Lulu. "But for today we'll just block out the dance."

It's a long lesson, but we learn quickly and soon we're able to move through most of the dance, pausing every now and then where an aerial will go. Before long, we're exhausted.

"Guess what I wore to school today?" I ask Ollie as we sit on the floor, having a break. I look pointedly at my feet.

"I'm disappointed about your hair."

"One step at a time," I say as the music starts, and Ollie stands, pulling me to my feet.

It's past 9:00 p.m. when Mum picks me up and takes me to the hospital.

Nan's in her own room in a part of the hospital for patients recovering from strokes. As we walk down the long, echoing corridor towards her room, Mum says, "She looks very ill. I want you to be prepared."

Well, obviously, I think. Outside her ward we squirt alcohol gel on our hands. I've been biting my nails and it stings.

She's lying back in a high bed, staring at a corner of the room. She doesn't have her teeth in or any makeup on, and her hair is limp and greasy. Her body and face look deflated. It's hard to see anything of Nan in the old lady lying on the bed. There's a horrible smell in the room, sort of sweet and warm. I fix my face to hide my shock.

"Hi, Nan," I say, giving her a kiss on her cheek, then standing back. Really, I want to climb up next to her on the bed and rest my head on her, like I did when I was a little girl. I want to tell her how last night was the worst night of my life, and how it's changed something in me. But I can't do this because she's covered in needles and tubes and she's just staring at me without smiling. After a couple of minutes, she seems to recognize me.

"Beatrice," she says, as though she is trying out the word. "I had an operation." Her voice is slurred.

"I know, Nan. I was so worried."

"When are the finals?" she interrupts me.

"Two weeks."

"You'll win," she says, and then she tries to smile.

"Thanks, Nan."

"Tell me about it." This comes out as a whisper.

So while Mum does lots of nursey things, I sit next to her bed, holding her hand—trying to ignore the needle held in place with tape and the splatters of brown blood—and tell her all about the semifinals. Nan stares at me without talking or smiling, which is strange at first, but then I get used to it.

Before we go, Mum explains that Dad isn't coming home for a few more weeks because she's out of the danger period and they really need him on the set. I'm sure she must be disappointed, but her face doesn't change from her blank expression.

She's falling asleep as I say good-bye. "Nan, will you come and watch the finals being filmed?" I ask.

"That would be lovely," she manages, but we both know it won't happen.

At home I sit in my room. I've been wanting Nan out of here so badly, but now she's gone it feels so quiet. Without thinking what I'm doing, I pick up my phone and call Kat. She answers immediately.

"Hey, Bea," she says, sounding uncertain. "What's up?"

"Bad stuff," I say. Then I tell her about Nan having a stroke and how terrible she looked tonight. I know nothing's going to change and that Kat's still going to dance with Pearl, but she's one of the only people who will understand how I feel right now. We talk for a while, never mentioning Pearl or *Starwars*.

"You looked amazing on TV," she says. "You and Ollie were perfect together." Her voice is flat. Is she jealous? Has she forgotten why I'm dancing with him? "I'd better go," she says after a moment. "Some of us have school in the morning."

We say good-bye and I drop my phone on my bed. I look around my room. So many things remind me of Kat: a photo of us dressed as Alice in Wonderland and the Cheshire Cat on World Book Day (I had to be the cat of course), the hamster she gave me for my birthday that sings "Kung Foo Fighting," and even a lipstick kiss that she put on my *Twilight* poster.

Will we ever talk on the phone again? Maybe it's time I accepted Kat and I are over.

The next few days are a blur of jive and hand gel as I rehearse, visit Nan in hospital and fit in a bit of school as well.

Everyone has heard about The Pink Ladies and Jive Monkey getting through to the finals, and in assembly Mrs. Pollard instructs each year group to "Watch *Starwars* on the TV and support your fellow students!" On Thursday, the local paper turns up and we get taken out of lessons for a photo on the field. The six of us stand shivering in a line waiting to be told what to do.

"Right, can you do something for me?" asks the woman holding the camera. We all look at her blankly until she adds, "You know, how you start or finish your dances, something that will look good in a photo." We separate into our two groups, or, rather, Ollie leaves his position next to Pearl and comes next to me. We stand in the close hold, and The Pink Ladies, directed by Pearl, strike an elaborate pose.

"Wonderful!" says the photographer. "Now, you two on the end, the Monkeys, I want you on your own. Do something different."

Still in the close hold, Ollie looks at me and frowns. It's hard for us to pick out a single move from the dance as each step flows into the next. Suddenly, his face lights up and he dips me backwards so my leg flies up in the air, then he turns and grins at the camera.

"Loving it!" the photographer calls out, snapping away. "Right, girls, I want you over by the sign to the school."

Ollie eases me back upright. "What was *that*?" I ask, laughing.

"I don't know," he says, looking panicked. "I thought it looked like the sort of move they do in old films, you know, at the end of the dance. Do you think it looked OK?"

"Well, we'll find out on Saturday."

Sure enough, when the paper comes out, there we are on the front page. I'm staring up at Ollie with what appears to be a look of adoration on my face, but I know it's really a look of shock. The Pink Ladies have a much smaller photo on page four.

Ha!

My heart lifts when I see Nan sitting up in bed sucking a drink with a straw. It's full of clinky ice cubes.

"Just tonic water, I'm afraid"—her voice is still a bit slurred—"but *this* is better than gin." She holds up a button attached to a tube and gives it a couple of clicks. "Morphine," she explains.

I show her my Marks & Spencer shopping bags. "I got everything you asked for." Tonight is *Starwars* night, and she's planned another party, but this time it's in hospital. "And I brought this to show you." I pass her a copy of the local paper.

"Beatrice! It's beautiful." Nan gazes in awe at the photo of Ollie and me, posing in our school uniforms. "Find my nail scissors. I want you to cut it out and stick it on the wall where I can see it." I'm still cutting out the picture when a nurse arrives.

"Hello, my love, did you buzz me?" she asks, pressing a button and turning off the flashing light over Nan's door.

"Yes, Trish. I wanted to show you this beautiful photo of my granddaughter in the papers."

"Nan," I groan. "She's too busy for that!" But the nurse doesn't seem to mind. She has a look at the photo and says that Ollie's got "the body of a swimmer" and is he my boyfriend?

"No," I say quickly.

"Well, you make a gorgeous couple," says Trish, which is a sweet lie, and the sort of thing nurses are good at saying. "Patients permitting, I'll be back to watch *Starwars* with you. After all, I did get my invitation!" She pulls a piece of paper out of her pocket and waves it as she leaves the room.

"Invitation?" I say. "Nan . . . what have you done?"

"I got Marion to make them for me—look." She finds a flyer-sized piece of paper next to her bed and hands it to me. I have to admit, Marion's not done a bad job. She's cut and pasted the *Starwars* logo at the top and below it is a picture of me, my body cropped from a Christmas Day photo. I know this, because I'm wearing a paper hat. In Comic Sans are the words: **Share a cup of tea and slice of cake with me, and watch my beautiful granddaughter jive her socks off. 8 p.m., Room 14, Friston Ward.** There is a border of stars around the whole thing and Marion has colored in some of the stars with a yellow felt-tip.

"You must be really proud of me," I say, staring at the invitation. I can't look at her.

"Bea, I've been this proud of you from the moment I set eyes on you." She picks up my hand. I know what's coming next. I've heard this story so many times. "I opened the front door, and there you were in your mum's arms, this tiny baby staring up at me with huge eyes." She smiles at the memory. "You looked so determined, so brave, I knew you could do *anything* you wanted."

"I might not win, Nan."

"Of course you will, Bea."

There's a knock at the door. It's the Polish man who hands round the tea and he's holding an invitation. It looks like our first guest has arrived. I look down again at the invitation and peer closer at the photo.

Hang on, what am I wearing?

"Nan, did you give Marion your phone and tell her to choose a photo?"

"That's right. I'd probably have chosen a different one. Her eyesight is shocking."

It's certainly an interesting picture. Last Christmas, Dad bet me a fiver that I couldn't fit in Emma's cat costume, and I proved that I could. It was made of Lycra and I managed to squeeze myself into it. Nan took a photo and it was so funny I sent it to Kat. Afterwards, they had to cut me out of it . . . Emma was not impressed. "How many of these did you give out, Nan?"

"Oh, around twenty?" She sounds vague. Ollie must *never* see this picture.

Soon, I'm crammed into the tiny room with Nan, two nurses, tea-man Antoni, Dr. Prosser and Marion, getting ready for my second-ever TV appearance. As the theme music starts, I feel the excitement grow in the room. There's a party atmosphere, helped by the sandwiches and cakes that are arranged on the bed. More people squeeze in to eat treats and see what all the fuss is about. I perch on the edge of Nan's bed, squeezing her hand, and when Ollie and I eventually appear on the screen everyone cheers, and I grip Nan's hand even tighter.

The nurses "oooh" and "aaah" throughout our dance and even though everyone knows we're through to the finals, they still clap and cheer when Shad reads out our names. Of course, Nan loves it when I say that she got us dancing together and as the credits roll she tells me she feels better than she has since her operation. Still, it's clear she's exhausted: Her skin is gray and she's finding it hard to talk. I wonder how many morphine clicks she had to help her get through this evening.

The room empties and I'm the last to go.

"Bea," she calls as I'm leaving. I stick my head back into the room again. She's sunk down in her pillows. "OK. Off you go. I just wanted to see those big brave eyes again."

13.

"You're one of the Jive Monkeys, aren't you?" says a woman by the tinned fruit. "I saw you on TV!" She says this nice and loud so everyone around us turns to stare. Mum's sent me down to the store before school to buy some milk and I've been spotted. "Can I have your photo?"

I pose for a photo and then she takes another one with us together. "OK, bye, Jive Monkey. Good luck!" she yells as I walk down the aisle.

If I thought this was strange, then school is much weirder. I am showered with attention. Usually, teachers struggle to remember my name. I get lots of "Um, you with the brown hair, Beth? Katie? Ellie? Don't tell me . . ." at which point I put them out of their misery and then they go, "That's it, Bea! Can you read from page twenty-six?"

Well, today, it's all . . . Hand these out, *Bea* . . . Pick a team, *Bea* . . . Hold my mint tea while I open the door, *Bea*.

By the time I get to rehearsal, I've signed two autographs, been kissed by an old man (I think he recognized me off TV) and had "You suck, Dance Monkey!" shouted by a man out of a car window. I smile sweetly and wave back. Ha! He'll have to try much harder than that to upset me . . . Pearl's toughened me up!

With just one week until the finals, Ollie and I are now rehearsing for longer than ever, often not finishing until ten. We are all over the new dance, and know it's looking good, but there is one ~~tiny~~ HUGE problem: I *still* can't do any aerial moves.

Today, even Lulu's starting to panic. "Look, if you two can't figure this out, you can't win—simple as that." She looks down at us on the floor where we've fallen once again. "Without it, the routine has no wow factor. It's just a well-executed jive that anyone could perform with enough practice and tuition. If you can master a basic aerial, like the knickerbocker, then all the others will follow. It will look stunning. If you can't, well, it will just look . . ."

She leaves us to imagine how tragic it will look . . . in

front of millions of viewers. We look away from each other as she tells us off. It's hopeless. Ray and Lulu have tried everything, but, when it comes to the vital moment, I just can't turn over beyond a certain point. "Bea, tell me honestly, why do you think Ollie will let you fall?"

What can I say? Each time we attempt an aerial I tell myself that this is it, this time it will work, I just have to follow Lulu's instructions, launch myself into Ollie's arms and trust him not to drop me. Everything is fine, then, at the crucial moment, I hesitate for a fraction of a second and I crash down.

Why don't I trust Ollie? *Pearl.* Ollie likes Pearl. How can he like the person whose hobby is hating me? Maybe it wouldn't matter if I didn't like him so much. But I do. I like him. I *totally* like him. Obviously, I can't tell Lulu this. In fact, I feel my eyes welling up. I look away. "I don't know," I say.

She looks exhausted. "OK. We're all tired. But, whatever it is, I want it figured out by tomorrow. We might as well call it a day."

She goes to help Ray dismantle the sound system.

Ollie and I remain on the floor.

"Oh, well," he says. He's lying back with his hands under his head, staring at the ceiling.

"I'm sorry."

"Maybe we'll be able to do it tomorrow." He gets up.

"Right, I'd better go or I'll be late." He looks at his phone, not at me.

I need to say something, explain what is worrying me and ask him about Pearl, but, really, it's none of my business. He is my dance partner, *not* my boyfriend. If I ask him how he can bear to spend time with a girl like Pearl, he'll know in an instant I like him. And not just his shoulders, all of him: eyes, arms, smile, even his backpack with the "Birthday Girl!" badge on it.

And that's the one thing he can never know, because then I won't even be able to dance with him.

When I look up, he has gone.

As I stand at the bus stop the next morning, I feel small and useless. The bus pulls up; I hold out my pass and climb on board.

Suddenly, Ollie stands in my way. "Sorry, wrong bus," he says to the driver, grabbing me by my sleeve and pulling me back on the pavement.

"What're you doing?" I ask. Then I notice he's wearing jeans. "Oh, God. It's non-school-uniform day . . . I didn't know!"

"Bea," he says, laughing, "stop worrying for *one* second. It's not non-school-uniform day. I'm skipping and so are you."

"What?"

"We can't do aerials because you don't trust me. Simple as that. I don't know why. But that's what I realized last night." He looks happy as he says this. "So I decided: Today we're going to have such a great day that when we go into rehearsals this afternoon you *will* trust me."

"That's crazy." *He was thinking about me last night?*

"Maybe . . . is your mum home?"

"No," I say, allowing myself to be pulled back in the direction of my house.

"Good, you need to get changed. Also, we need to call school and say why we're not in, otherwise they call home."

"Where are we going?"

"The seaside!"

I know, I know, I should insist on going to school. This could get me into deep trouble and if Mum finds out it will be another stressful event for her to cope with. But I don't say no. Instead I say, "I love the seaside!"

Half an hour later, we're sitting on a bus heading for Brighton. Speaking with my best "lady" voice, I tell the school secretary that unfortunately my son, Ollie Matthews, has once again "got that nasty rash he picks up at rugby training . . . and it's very itchy."

Five minutes later, Ollie calls up and tells them that

his daughter, Beatrice Hogg, has been so sick "it's coming out of her nose."

We sit on our own on the top deck of the bus and creep towards the coast, stopping at each town on the way. To start off with, I'm terrified that we'll be spotted by a teacher—at school, I have never even had a detention.

"This is the naughtiest thing I've done in my whole life," I explain.

Ollie rolls his eyes. "Well then it's time you did some naughty things."

Still, my stomach churns and it's only when we get off the bus and are swallowed up in the packed streets of Brighton that I relax and start to enjoy myself. I even forget about my horrible coat that Mum refuses to replace and the way the wind is puffing up my hair and giving me a Marge Simpson.

First, we go to the pier and play on the slot machines. Ollie dedicates half an hour—and around two hundred twopence—to winning a plastic key ring with a French sausage on it. At least, we hope it's a sausage. It's wearing a beret and carrying a baguette, so it's definitely French. We race motorbikes, but Ollie refuses to go again with me because I beat him, although he claims it's because I "scream like a bunking schoolgirl."

Finally, because our money is going fast, we go on a game called Dance Dance Revolution Supernova II and jump around on lit-up plastic squares and "move and groove in time to the beat." The machine's verdict is "ass." Ollie's convinced the lights on the display are broken and it should say "Badass" . . . I'm not so sure.

We wander along the walk and get some fries, eating them on the pebbly beach, throwing one or two to the seagulls that are lurking around. Behind us, the wind snaps the sails of dinghies that have been pulled up the shore, and ropes slap against masts. The sky is Disney-cartoon blue and the sun warms my face.

We watch as people fight to control blowing newspapers, play the bongos, argue, cuddle and eat. We don't need to talk. I let my mind drift back to Pearl and start to get tied up in knots thinking about how she'll respond to me sitting on the beach with her boyfriend . . . after all, they are going out, aren't they?

I look at Ollie and realize that he's looking at me. Then I have a revelation: Why don't I ask him?

"Ollie, are you and Pearl going out?" My moment of mad fierceness leaves me and I feel my cheeks burn. He screws up his face and looks out to sea. Surely this is a "yes" or "no" answer. It can't be that difficult!

"Ah . . . well . . . no. I suppose we were *seeing* each other, for about five minutes, but then she did something and I told her we should just be friends. You remember, that time I was late for rehearsal?"

"I remember," I say, thinking back to my big snotty tears in the car.

"That's when I told her, or tried to tell her, but she wouldn't listen. I suppose I should say what she did." As he talks he starts to throw stones in my empty paper cup. "It's funny really that such a small thing should bother me so much. She said my dog, Stan, looked like a *retard*. There was other stuff too, but I hate that word and I love my dog, and once she said it I realized that was it."

I join him in the stone throwing. "Well, Stan's in good company," I say. "She's always calling me a retard . . . and a fat weirdo ugly rat, but not all at the same time . . . well, she did once."

"Oh . . . that's not good," says Ollie. "Stan got it easy. For the record, Bea, you're not a fat weirdo ugly rat."

"Thanks, Ollie, that's sweet." This makes him laugh.

"Hey, anytime." He shakes out the cup and puts it a bit farther away. "But, seriously, there's something not right about Pearl. She can get so angry . . . and aggressive. Have you told her where to go?"

"I'm building up to it, but she's scary and, well, I'm clearly *not*."

"No. You're like the anti-Pearl. She can be fun, nice even, on her own."

"I know."

Ollie looks surprised.

I explain, "We used to be friends . . . In fact, when I was seven, I believe I would have described her as a *best* friend." This is clearly news to him. "We were in a pretty tough girl-gang called the Ladybirds. Pearl made up our secret wave!"

"Show me." I hold up my hand and tuck my thumb in. Then I wiggle my fingers.

"You see, four fingers, four Ladybirds: me, Kat, Betty and Pearl."

"Hard to imagine," he says. "Hey, do you remember my party?" I can tell that he wants to set the record straight. "Well, she dragged me upstairs 'to talk,' then trapped me in my room for half an hour, crying and telling me why I *had* to go out with her before passing out on the carpet. When I got downstairs, you'd gone."

Relief floods through me, the sun shines brighter and the fries taste amazing.

"I thought you were more than friends," I say.

"Well, she's very *touchy-feely*," Ollie says. Ha! *The* understatement of the year. "And I think she needs a friend . . . but, Bea, I didn't know she was saying those things to you."

I stare at the sea. It wasn't just the things she said, it was the looks, the texts, the pasta in the hair—everything. I decide that now isn't the time to go into all that. Ollie is *not* going out with Pearl. The sun is shining. We are together.

"I've suddenly realized something," I say, turning to look at him. "I'm fine . . . everything is fine . . . I'm not even worried about the final." He looks at me with his kind, smiling eyes, trying to work out if I'm telling the truth, and I can't quite believe that I, Bea Hogg, am here with *the* Ollie Matthews. "Do you know what we should do?"

"What?"

"Go on that." I point at a ride right on the end of the pier. It's a giant roller coaster, and its track twists and turns high in the sky and over the sea. "The Crazy Mouse," I say, reading the name that flashes in letters on the side.

"Come on, then," says Ollie, pulling me to my feet and dragging me up the pebbles. I say "dragging" but there may be the tiniest possibility that he is holding my hand. A few seconds later, he lets go, but my fingers are still tingling when the safety bar locks us into the Crazy Mouse.

We fly round in circles, the cars shooting off the edge of the pier only to be whipped back in at the last moment. I *love* fast rides, but it turns out that Ollie doesn't. He buries his head in his arms for the whole three minutes and just repeats, "Oh no oh no oh no," not appreciating any of my "the people look like ants!" comments.

Knowing that Ollie *doesn't* love my bully makes him less mysterious, and as we wander around Brighton's odd little shops, I feel like I belong at his side. When he looks at his phone, I don't assume he's desperate for a friend to call and save him from the boredom of spending time with dull Bea Hogg: He is just checking the time. When he goes quiet, he probably isn't thinking about how repulsive the zit on my forehead is, or how my coat was clearly bought for me by a mum on a very tight budget . . . he's just, well, not talking.

Before we get the bus home, Ollie buys us a milk shake from the café where you pick your own flavors. He lets me choose. Strawberry cheesecake and Milky Way: the perfect end to a perfect day.

Ollie and I get the bus back in time for our rehearsal, in fact, we're early, which makes Lulu narrow her eyes. We're in such a good mood, and so excited to get going, that she gives us the benefit of the doubt and accepts that school *has* shut twenty minutes early because the toilets have broken, *and* it's a non-uniform day.

"We have a week of rehearsals left, less than that. Today you *have* to do an aerial move or we're taking them all out," says Lulu in a voice that doesn't match her weenie height or bouncing braids.

"We can do it," says Ollie. Ray puts on our final's song, "Sing, Sing, Sing," and Ollie and I move through the dance, building up to our first aerial: the moonflip. He pulls me close, puts both hands on my waist and I jump. He swings me higher and higher, over and around his shoulder. We reach the point where I normally tumble to the floor but, today, it's effortless: Ollie's arms are steel and his hands grip me firmly as I fly round. The world spins and then my feet land surely, but as soft as a feather, on wooden floorboards.

We freeze, Ollie's hands still on my waist. Lulu grins, and with a massive whoop, Ray leaps off the stage.

"We did it," says Ollie, amazed. He gives my waist a squeeze. "We did it!" Then he frowns. "What's the matter?"

I clutch my hand to my mouth and feel the blood drain from my face. "Oh, no," I gasp, then I pull away from him and rush from the hall. I make it to the toilet just in time. The skipping, the fries, the Crazy Mouse, the truth about Pearl and the cheesecake milk shake were all shaken up when Ollie flipped me upside down. I'm sick, *really* sick, but even as Lulu rushes in and holds my hair back from my face I manage to smile and say, "We did it, didn't we? Was it good?"

"It was perfect."

Having gargled with water about twenty times and quickly chewed half a pack of Ray's gum, I sheepishly wander back into the hall. After promising Lulu I feel fine, our practice continues.

"That was pretty funny," says Ollie. "But maybe don't do it on live TV?"

"Right," interrupts Ray, "remember, all aerials are dangerous, so concentrate. One mistake can result in serious injury."

"Or serious barfing."

"Shut up, Ollie."

"OK."

Lecture over, we get down to the hard work—learning all those aerial moves that have been out of our reach: the moonflip, knickerbocker, pancake, chuck and judo flip. To think I used to worry about holding Ollie's *hand*. The rehearsal is like twister for two, with added music, and I don't even blush when Lulu says, "Lift her butt, Ollie, come on! Squeeze her into the lift," and, "Press into his chest, Bea, you need the momentum." It's at moments like these, that I really miss Kat, although Ollie's a surprisingly good substitute.

Lulu yells, "Lock on to his crotch, Bea! Lock on!" and Ollie laughs so hard we have to stop dancing.

We're jubilant when we leave the hall, a bit earlier than usual because all the acrobatics have knocked it out of us. We wander down the road before standing on the corner where we usually go our separate ways.

"So, see you at school," I say. "And thank you for introducing me to naughty ways . . . the skipping, I mean."

"I think we got away with it. Even if we get found out, it was worth it."

There's a moment of silence and Ollie looks at me with a frown. It's getting closer to summer and the days are getting longer. It is one of those beautiful evenings when the wind dies away and the light becomes soft. Some kids are out playing on their scooters. As we stand there, facing each other, their screams fade into the distance. Ollie continues to look at me and, all of a sudden, we seem to be standing *very* close together indeed.

"I loved today," I say in a rush. And then I ruin everything by adding, "Except the puking." Well, that breaks the spell.

Ollie grins and we take a step back.

"See you, Bean." He gives me a wave, turns round and walks down the road.

I watch the back of his head for a moment, the slope of his shoulders as he pushes his hands into his pockets, then I turn and walk back home.

I don't just love his shoulders. I love all of him. So this is what it feels like—love. Amazing . . . and a little bit terrifying. I rein myself in. How tragic. Just because Ollie isn't going out with Pearl there's no reason why he'd suddenly want to go out with scared, shy, wrong-shaped Bea Hogg from the ninth grade.

But then it hits me.

I'm not so shy—or scared, anymore. And I'm not the wrong shape. In fact, I'm the perfect shape. Maybe I

should start thinking of myself as happy, confident, cur-
vaceous Bea Hogg . . . of the ninth grade (I can't do much
about that) who's a kick-ass jiver. That sounds much more
like girlfriend material.

So, for once, I let myself fantasize about being Ollie's
girlfriend. And you know those moments in Disney films?
When the bluebirds start tweeting and the princess holds
her skirts out and twirls around a meadow and sings?
That's how I feel.

15.

"**F**eeling better, Bea?" asks Mr. Simms the next morning, which makes me feel bad for a second, then I remember I was *actually* sick so, in a way, I'm not lying.

In my quietest voice, I tell Betty all about the day Ollie and I spent in Brighton, leaving out a few important details, you know, the ones to do with bluebirds and *love*. Even so, she looks at me slyly and says, "You two are taking the whole 'partner' thing really seriously." I'm saved from having to say anything back by the register being called, but Betty keeps smiling to herself and looking at me out of the corner of her eye. I shake my head like she's a big fool, which she is, but this just makes her grin even more.

I'm treated to almost a week of Pearl-free days at

school as The Pink Ladies go into dance overdrive. Each
night, Ollie and I are similarly immersed in rehearsals,
practicing the aerials again and again. By Thursday, we
can moonflip, knickerbocker, pancake, chuck and judo
flip with ease . . . and without me puking.

On Friday, I'm standing in the lunch line, running
through the hand signal to the moonflip in my head,
when my thoughts are interrupted by Pearl's voice. With
Lauren, she pushes to the front of the line and begins
telling some seventh grade girl to "lend" her a pound.
With Pearl standing over her, the girl opens up her purse
and looks inside. The thing that really gets to me is the
purse. It's shaped like a ladybird. For some reason, that
makes what Pearl is doing even worse. The girl looks
scared. In fact, her hands are trembling so much she
can't get any money out.

"I've only got enough for my lunch," she says in a
whisper.

"Oh well," says Pearl, snatching the purse and taking
the money. "Ta." She drops the empty purse back into the
girl's hands. The girl stands behind Pearl, trying and
failing to zip it up.

My body is shaking. I'm furious. I leave my place in
the line and walk up to them.

"What d'you want?" asks Pearl.

"I want *you* to give that girl her money back," I say, trying to keep my voice calm as Pearl's clear blue eyes stare at me.

"What?"

"Give her back her money." Pearl laughs, so I carry on, "What makes you think you can take someone else's money from them?" The anger is showing now in my voice and this makes her laugh even more. Lauren smiles nervously.

"She *lent* it to me, you retard," says Pearl, using *that* word. Then she turns round and says, "Didn't you!" to the girl with the ladybird purse. The girl nods and stares at the ground, probably hating me for getting involved and making everything worse.

Pearl turns back to face me, leans forward and says, "*See.* So why don't you mind your own business, you silly little bitch?" she says the last three words quietly and without emotion, almost like they are my name. Then she turns away as though another little problem has been sorted out.

I give her a shove on her back. I have to force myself to do it gently because I am feeling very fierce. Pearl spins round. "She doesn't want to give you her money. You forced her to. You *steal* from seventh graders. I can cope with you calling me 'silly' and 'little,' but 'bitch'?" Without realizing it, I have begun to shout and I step closer to her. "That is *you*, Pearl—you are one *massive* bitch, probably the biggest bitch in the school. And I am SICK of it!" I point at the girl's purse. "A *ladybird*, Pearl . . . what's happened to you?" I'm really shouting now and, although I know it sounds massively uncool, I just can't stop my voice from rising until finally I yell, "Now give her back her pound!"

The cafeteria is silent and Pearl stands there staring at me, her glossy mouth hanging open. Then she composes herself, blinks her big, beautiful eyes, sucks in her breath, pulls back her arm and throws the pound coin—very hard—at my face.

"There you are," she says calmly, before turning and walking out of the cafeteria with Lauren trotting after her.

The coin has hit me in the corner of my eye. I clutch my face. A few seconds later, the pain dies down and I take away my hands. My whole face throbs and I can't see properly through my blurry eye. Stretching my arms out, I feel around on the floor until I find the coin and I give it to the girl. The cafeteria is still, deadly silent.

"Thanks," says the girl, taking the coin and putting it back in her ladybird purse. "Your eye's bleeding."

Trying to walk as normally as possible and ignoring the stares, I find my bag and leave the cafeteria. As I go, the talking starts again. I make my way towards the bathroom. I have to look in a mirror and see what damage Pearl has done. Suddenly, a blurred figure stands in front of me.

"Bea, what happened?" It's Ollie. I'd recognize his voice anywhere.

"I got a pound in my eye," I say, laughing, although tears of pain run down my cheeks. He holds both of my hands, something that feels strange, even though we have done it for hours and hours in rehearsals. "How?"

"Pearl threw it at me . . . It's a long story."

"You need to go to the nurse. I don't think you can walk."

"I can walk."

"No, we'll make a chair for you."

By now, Betty has appeared and they cross over their arms to make a seat and lift me up. I rest my arms round their shoulders while they run, very recklessly, down the corridor yelling at people to get out of the way. By the time, we get to the nurse's room, I'm laughing so much that I feel fine. She still makes me lie down with a packet of peas on my face.

"Don't eat them," says Ollie.

They ask the nurse if they can stay with me and miss their next class, but she pushes them out.

"You've got two very silly friends there," she tells me. I

smile behind the bag of peas and, although I know it's crazy, I feel really, really happy.

When I walk out of school at the end of the day, all that's left to show for the pound coin incident is a tiny cut and a larger purple bruise. I've had one lesson with Pearl and she's been strangely quiet, not even whispering to her best friends about me. I suppose I'd describe it as an icy silence, but it's definitely an improvement. The funny thing is, even though she's actually hit me, I'm not scared of her anymore. I don't avoid looking in her direction, or lower my voice when I talk to Betty. She is losing her powers.

I walk across the playground and notice Ollie leaning on the wall by the gate. I prepare to do our usual nod and smile as I pass by, but he leaves his friends and walks over.

"Hello," he says. "You do know you've got a black eye, don't you?"

"Does it look that bad?"

"You could wear an eye patch." He falls into step beside me. "Lulu's probably got a vintage one with cherries on it."

"The nurse promised me they could cover it up with makeup."

"Hmm," says Ollie doubtfully.

As we walk to rehearsal, I tell Ollie what happened in

the cafeteria, exaggerating a little for comic effect. If it had happened a couple of months ago, pre-Ollie and pre-jive, I'd have been devastated.

Ollie listens, then says, "Well done, Bea."

"What for?"

"Sticking up for that girl. Those were the actions of a fierce jive monkey."

"They were, weren't they?" I say.

Our rehearsal finishes at eight when Lulu says: "That's it. That's as good as it's going to get."

They're all going to get pizza and ask me along, but I'm going to see Nan. I've accepted that there's no way she's going to make it to the finals tomorrow and I need to speak to her.

When I arrive, she's staring at the door like she's been waiting for me. Quickly, she arranges her face into a big smile, hiding the discomfort she's obviously feeling.

"So, Beatrice, this is it."

I go and sit next to her. The bed is so high my legs dangle over the side. "I wish you could come and watch," I say. All of a sudden, *Starwars*, dancing, even Ollie, it all seems unreal. To see Nan, who is usually full of life, stuck in a hospital bed surrounded by beeps and wires, this is real.

"I wish I could come too, more than anything."

"It's thanks to you, Nan, all this."

"I said that you'd love jive." She gives my hand a squeeze. I notice that all her nail polish has chipped off.

"No, not just the dancing," I say, "*everything*." Nan frowns. "When you got ill, I thought I'd never get the chance to tell you, but dancing has changed my life. I'm happy now. I thought I was before, but I kept the real me hidden away, especially at school. I would never have believed I could learn to jive, but you knew I could do it."

"Bea, you can do *anything*. You are a strong young woman . . . and you're *my* granddaughter." And I know Nan doesn't want me to say any more gushy stuff so, carefully avoiding her tangle of heart, blood pressure and temperature monitors, I lie next to her on the bed, rest my head on her pink knitted bed jacket and watch the end of *Downton Abbey*.

16.

"**G**osh, Bea, chive, chive, CHIVE," says a voice in my ear. I blink and jiggle up and down. What's going on? Then I have a "Christmas morning" moment of realization. This isn't any old Saturday . . . This is *Starwars* Saturday! Emma has been sent to wake me up and has chosen to do this by bouncing on my bed and showering me with sheets of paper. "Made you a picture," she says, her breath all Cocoa Puffy. She's being modest. She's made many pictures.

"It's great," I say, trying to focus on the one closest to my face. It's of Ollie and me dancing. I wouldn't know this if Mum hadn't helpfully labeled the large-headed blobs with our names. She's used a lot of red crayon and it looks like a murder on the dance floor. She gets into bed with me, bringing all her pictures with her.

"Why are you so sticky?" I ask.

"I painted me with chocolate spread," she says, licking her arm. "Bea want some?" I leap out of bed and head for the shower. Emma is the best alarm clock.

I do everything in a daze. I wash my hair, dry it, get dressed, eat the toast Mum has insisted on making me and check through my bag. Mum's coming up to London this afternoon and Marion will be taking Emma into the hospital so they can watch me on TV with Nan.

Mum keeps giving me hugs and asking annoying questions like, "Do you think you should take a spare pair of underwear?" (no!) and, "Will I embarrass you if I wear my plunge bra?" (yes!) and "Can I run onstage if you win?" (you probably won't have to worry about that one), and I'm relieved when Lulu turns up.

Emma shrieks, "Holly! Holly!" and dives into the car, climbing on Ollie's knee and clinging to his leg. I climb in after her and pull her off him. She transfers her affection to me and wraps her arms round my neck demanding, "A big French kiss!"

"Don't worry," I say to Ollie. "It's not as bad as it sounds." I hold Emma's face between my hands and then shower her with kisses on both her cheeks, continental-style. Satisfied, she lets Mum lift her out of the car.

"This is it, Bean," he says.

"It certainly is, Holly." As we pull away from the curb, we both wave to Mum and Emma, who is being restrained in her arms.

Lulu is driving us up because, now we're finalists, we're worthy of parking at the studios. Ray has come along too and Lulu puts on some rock and roll, and he sings along as we cruise down the motorway. Ollie and I stare out of the window, make the odd *make sure you do this* comment, and I start to get a really, really, pukey feeling in my stomach.

"Apparently," says Lulu, cutting Ray off in the middle of "Bim Bam Baby," "lots of pubs in town are going to be showing the finals and hosting *Starwars* parties. I saw it on the news last night. Everyone wants you to win." That's a lot of pressure. I imagine angry drunks throwing chips at my face on a big screen after I screw up the pancake.

As we drive into London, we fall silent, and when the Big Town Playboys sing "The Wobble" I think we all know what they mean. Too soon, we're pulling up at the security gates and being directed to our parking space.

It's all a bit different from the semifinals. This time, Gem greets us by name and we're taken to our very own dressing room. Admittedly, it's tiny—just a box room with a sink, sofa and lots of mirrors—but it has "Jive Monkey" on the door (with stars around it), which Lulu makes us pose by for a photo. We're told not to get changed because first we rehearse and they want our hair and makeup perfect for filming.

Lulu and Ray disappear to the hospitality room with all the other chaperones and Ollie and I are taken to an empty studio where all the finalists have gathered.

As Gem stands up to talk, the door opens and The Pink Ladies come in looking unusually flustered. I look at Kat, but she turns away from me. Her cheeks are red. She's been crying.

"Find a seat, girls. Right, listen up because I've got a lot to tell you," says Gem, and she explains exactly what we will be doing for the rest of the day.

From her position on the floor, Pearl scans the room, presumably looking for Ollie. When she sees where we're sitting, she smiles and mouths, "Hi!"

I go to turn away, then look back. Pearl is staring straight at *me*, waving. Automatically, I wave back. *What is going on?* Then I let my hand drop down and turn back to concentrate on what Gem is saying.

"Right, in a moment, you're going to go back to your dressing rooms and then you're all going to have the chance to rehearse in this studio," she says. "You won't be watching each other because we don't want any of you being put off or getting last-minute jitters."

Ollie smiles, knowing Gem's words will automatically

give me last-minute jitters. "Food will be brought to your dressing rooms, but I'm afraid there's going to be quite a lot of sitting around. I hope you don't get too bored. Right, off you go."

The first group stays in the room and the rest of us leave. The Pink Ladies wait by the door.

"Hi, guys!" says Pearl giving us both a big smile. "Oh my God, we are, like, sooo nervous. How d'you feel?"

I look at Kat—she must know just how odd this is. She's looking better, but her eyes are still red. Holly and Lauren start chatting to me too. Clearly, it's now "allowed." Even Ollie notices the difference and gives me a questioning look.

"Hey," says Pearl, as we walk down the corridor. "Did that girl say when we're getting our makeup done?"

"As soon as we've rehearsed," replies Ollie. "Hopefully, they'll be able to sort out Bea's black eye." Silence falls, and he looks steadily at Pearl.

She hesitates then seems to come to a decision. "Oh! Look, babe"—she steps forward and puts her arm round me—"let's forget about all that." Then she squeezes me to her, smothering me in her perfume. "Yeah?"

By now we're outside our dressing room. I know that the easiest thing to do is say, "Yeah, OK!" and six weeks ago that's exactly what I would have done, but that girl isn't me anymore. I pull away from her. "Do you want me to forget about the coin?" I say. "Or about everything? The drawing you did of me, the photo you took, what you said at the party, the texts? You see, that's a lot to *forget* about." I say this as calmly as I can.

Pearl looks at me, trying to decide what to do. She expected me to be grateful, relieved to be given the opportunity to be her friend. Holly's mouth hangs open, amazed that I'm passing up this once-in-a-lifetime opportunity.

"God," Pearl says, that familiar cold voice creeping back in. "What *is* your problem?"

"Yeah, Bea, Pearl's trying to sort everything out. You're not being fair," adds Lauren.

So now *I* am being cruel to Pearl. I suddenly feel totally exhausted by the weeks and weeks of having to be constantly on guard, waiting to see what Pearl will say or do next. I screw up my toes in my shoes and shut my eyes for a second, trying to get to a point where I can sound normal.

"Stop it," says Kat, quietly. "This is what I was talking about, Pearl. Why can't we just do our dance? Why can't you leave Bea alone?"

It's as if Kat hasn't spoken. Pearl peers at me and says, "Ah, she's going to cry!" Life has rewound to the day on the bus, the day that started all of this, when she was waving Emma's Barbie around, glitter and tea leaves falling on her nails, and I stood there and let her do it.

"I'm not going to cry," I say, surprised that it's true. "But I don't want to spend time with someone like you, Pearl."

I open the dressing-room door and walk in. Ollie follows me, shutting the door behind him. I sit down on the sofa and breathe deeply. He sits next to me and all of a sudden I realize that we're going to be on our own in this tiny room for three long hours. I become aware of everything about Ollie. I notice that his jeans are frayed and that his arm is resting across the back of the sofa. That he's half looking at me—he could be checking out the multicolored bruise that surrounds my eye, but I don't think he is. This is one small sofa we're sitting on.

"Are you cold?" he asks. I nod. I've left my jacket in Lulu's car and our dressing room has chilling air-conditioning. He passes his hoodie to me, the gray one with the fleecy lining, and I put it on. It smells of Ollie, warm and safe, and I have an urge to snuggle my face down into it and go, "Mmmm." Thankfully, I suppress this urge. Then he pulls a chair in front of us, kicks off his sneakers and puts his feet up, leaving room for mine. I slip off my shoes and put my feet next to his.

I'm wearing socks that have individual toes, sort of gloves for my feet. Actually, I didn't realize I had them on. I wear them around the house like slippers and, in the panic this morning, I forgot to change them. Each toe is knitted a different color and has a weird Japanese cartoon character on it—one of my dad's last-minute presents from abroad.

"Cool socks," says Ollie.

"Thanks." I wriggle my toes. "Same goes for yours. Is Bart *naked*?"

"Yep. They're my lucky socks," he replies, and we both stare at our feet, which are resting on the chair, inches apart. "Do you want to know something, Bea?"

"What?" I'm just thinking how funny life is, here I am in heaven when five minutes ago I was on the verge of tears.

"I really like your socks." And Ollie sort of strokes my toes with his feet. I stop breathing. I have fireworks in my toes and they're spreading through my whole body. I breathe again, but really quietly so that Ollie doesn't know his toes have the power to stop my breath. He leaves his foot just resting against mine.

Never in the history of the universe has the meeting of two socks felt so amazing.

"Do you want to know something else?" He has stopped looking at our toes and is now looking at me.

"What?" I whisper, staring intently at Bart's little yellow bum.

"I really like you," he says.

I repeat the words slowly in my head and I feel as

though I'm hovering at that point in the moonflip when I could fly on over or crash to the ground. I know that while I look at his toes I'm safe, but if I raise my eyes to look at him I'll find out what he means. Does he like me, or *like* me?

But I'm still far too shy to look at him. Instead, I do something incredibly fierce. I lean towards him and rest my head on his shoulder. It's something I've longed to do for weeks and it's even better than I imagined. There's a second when I'm not sure how he's going to react and I keep very still, waiting for my next clue. But he doesn't leap up off the sofa screaming, "Get off me!" Instead, he pulls me closer.

Keep breathing, Bea. Keep breathing. I find the courage I need to look at him. Our eyes meet for a second, we smile and then I go so red I have to bury my face back in his shoulder.

"Sorry, Ollie, I'm just too embarrassed to look at you right now."

Then, as if in slow motion, I sit up, he puts his other hand on the side of my face and, as smoothly as a perfectly executed dance move, our lips touch . . .

"Sandwiches!" The door is flung open and a man pulling a metal cart backs into the room.

Ollie and I leap off the sofa, our lips having only met for a fraction of a second. In fact, I'm not even sure if they met at all. "Now, what do you want? We've cheese and tomato, cheese and pickle, ham, oh, and cheese."

"That's a lot of cheese," says Ollie in a relatively normal voice as he studies the cart, choosing one of the paper plates and then passing one to me. "Here you go, Bea, your favorite: cheese and pickle."

And they are my favorite! I mentioned it once, weeks ago—I can't even remember why—and he has remembered. I feel as though I've been given a bunch of roses rather than a slightly stale sandwich wrapped in plastic. Just as the sandwich man is backing out of the room, Gem sticks her head in. "Don't eat those. Time for rehearsal and makeup."

My jive "look" requires a good hour in makeup and when I get back to our dressing room, I know Ollie must be inside. Self-consciously, I hover outside before opening the door and slipping into the room.

Ollie looks up from his phone. "Hello," he says. "Have you seen Bea Hogg, my dance partner?"

"Very funny," I say, perching on the edge of the sofa. I have been brushed and painted all over—even my shoulders have makeup on—and I hardly dare sit down.

"That is a serious amount of makeup," he laughs.

I look closer at him. "Are you wearing mascara?"

"Hey, she said she wanted to define my, quote, 'lush' eyes." We hesitate. I need to get changed, but I don't think one almost-kiss with Ollie has prepared me to strip down to my underwear and bra quite yet.

"Right, I'll wait outside," he says, like a gentleman. Nan would be impressed.

When I'm ready, I stand in front of a mirror. I have an entirely new outfit. *Starwars* took over our costumes for the finals and organized them with Lulu. We can't dance in jeans anymore because the routine is so acrobatic and, according to Lulu, skirts are "more fun" for aerials. Personally, I think they're more drafty, but here I am wearing a short flirty black skirt, a tight red shirt that fits me—and my boobs—like a glove, and not one, but *two* pairs of the most massive sports underwear ever.

I study my reflection and although I know I look just right, I still can't bring myself to open the door and show Ollie. Get a grip, Ladybird, millions of strangers are about to see your pants. I pull open the door. He's leaning on the wall opposite.

"I'm ready," I say. Well, obviously.

He comes back into the room and he looks at me in that way he has, totally open and relaxed. "Bean, you look beautiful." Yes. Beautiful. *That* is the word he just said. Bean + beautiful. I repeat it a few times to prolong the glow that is spreading over me. "Now," he says, "assume the close hold, but not too close, or you'll smudge my makeup."

"Are we practicing?" I ask as we do a miniature version of our dance—minus the aerial moves—around our dressing room.

"Sort of," he says, and we step around the room with Ollie providing the music. Hundreds of questions flash through my head involving the words *like, kiss, beautiful, boyfriend,* and *girlfriend,* but I don't ask any of them because I don't want anything to change.

Our dance finishes when Ollie's phone rings and it's not long before Gem pops her head round the door to let us know our families are here. "Less than an hour to go, guys!" she says as she leaves the room.

At eight, a speaker in the corner of our dressing room busts into life and we hear the *Starwars* theme tune. By now, we are both sitting on the sofa and staring at the wall. Although we can't actually *see* the first dancers, we can hear their music, Shad's commentary and the audience's reactions. This has the same effect as a slow drum roll.

Soon, a runner arrives to take us to warm up and, before we know it, we're backstage, holding hands and listening to the applause for the dancers who are leaving the stage. Gem holds up her hand and begins her countdown. Five, four, three, two . . . then she gives us a shove, and we run on.

Our music fills the studio as we enter the stage, find

our position, and step into the close hold. Out of the corner of my eyes, I see a blur of cameras, lights and faces. Then, a second later, we start our dance. At first the tempo is slow, very slow for a rock 'n' roll song, and we waltz in slow motion for a couple of seconds. I can feel our hearts beating as we force ourselves to keep the pace down. Then the music speeds up and so do we, flying into the moon-flip at a speed I never dreamt we'd achieve when we began to dance together.

We're so fast you can tell the audience isn't expecting me to spin over. We hear a collective gasp, then we're surrounded with cheers. Swinging through our solos and aerials, the audience responds to each stage of our dance until we're coming to our final lift.

I'm grinning as I turn up and over Ollie's shoulder where he holds me until the last beat of the track. He lowers me to the ground and we let the applause wash over us, holding hands, laughing and trying to get our breath back.

"How about *that*, ladies and gentlemen?" Shad runs over. The applause starts all over again. "Now, Ollie, you promised us something special, and you delivered it. How did you do it in such a short space of time?"

"Well, we have great teachers, my sister, Lulu, and Ray. They're here tonight"—through the glare of the spotlights I make out Lulu, waving at a camera right in front of her—"and I have an amazing partner."

There is a collective "ahhh!" from the audience.

"So, Bea, anyone you'd like to mention?"

"Just my nan. I wish you were here, Nan." Unlike Ollie, I don't have the ability to make up perfect sound bites on the spot.

"Great, so hello, Nan, and thank you, Jive Monkey—you were *spectacular!*" We run offstage to a final round of applause.

As we are one of the last acts, we don't have long to wait until everyone is brought back onstage. The Pink Ladies are at the opposite end to us and looking as nervous as everyone else. Shad welcomes back the viewers and begins to describe the wonderful opportunities that await the winners.

Ollie and I squeeze hands.

"Ladies and gentlemen, tonight there can only be *one* group who performs in the West End. The judges have made their decision. Dancers, if you hear your name read out, I would like you to take a step back: You have *not* won *Starwars.*" After an agonizing pause, he reads out the first name, "Bollywood! I'm sorry." The group of girls next to us draw in their breath and one of them gives a cry as she realizes that they haven't won. They stand back in the shadows beyond the reach of the spotlights.

Shad continues eliminating groups and Ollie and I hold hands so tightly I can't feel my fingers. "Bo Salsa!" With each name he pauses to allow the cameras time to film the disappointment on the dancers' faces. "The Follies! Element! The Pink Ladies!"

I hear Pearl gasp at the end of the row and then she shakes her head as the others hug by her side.

"Please take a step back," reminds Shad. They disappear from sight.

He reads out several more names, ending with Dance Collective. A drum rolls. "Ladies and gentlemen, we have *three* groups remaining." The stage is now almost empty except for two other groups. One is made up of five girls wearing tailored trousers and waistcoats. The other is a group of seriously athletic street dancers. "Kiss, No Angels and Jive Monkey, you are the acts our judges have been agonizing over. Unfortunately, there can only be *one* winner tonight . . ."

Shad pauses and takes a gold envelope out of his pocket, which he opens as the drum roll gets louder. "If I read out your name, you have *not* won *Starwars*."

I take a deep breath and shut my eyes.

"Kiss! I'm sorry!" The audience groans and claps. Relief surges through me and I open my eyes to see the girls wearing the waistcoats step back. "Jive Monkey and No Angels, there is *one* name on this card," says Shad, coming to stand in between us.

He pauses and takes a deep breath. "No Angels . . . *you* are our *Starwars* champions!"

It takes me a second to work out what has happened

and I stand there, staring into the distance, clutching Ollie's hand. A camera swings in front of my face and I look up at Ollie, vaguely aware that No Angels are going crazy somewhere over to my left. Ollie and I smile and he nods, telling me that I've got it right: We haven't won.

Then he puts his hand in my hair, pulls me closer and kisses me. I am so shocked I just fall against him and kiss him back, our fingers entwined, our hearts thudding. Applause, lights and cameras swirl around us as we melt into each other. Who would have thought losing could feel this amazing?

Finally, we have to step apart.

"Really?" I ask Ollie.

"Really," he says, smiling. Together, we turn to face No Angels, and then I grin and clap, and generally hide the fact that inside my mind is screaming, you, Bea Hogg, have just been kissed by the amazingly breathtakingly stunning Ollie Matthews . . . on live TV in front of ten million people!

Not bad for my first-ever kiss.

Pearl doesn't take the whole "kissing on TV" thing very well. In fact, backstage, she stands in front of Ollie with her hands on her hips, blocking our path.

"What are you thinking?" She's incredulous. "What do you see in *her*?"

Ollie looks at me thoughtfully, then turns back to

Pearl. "Well, she's got great timing and a good sense of rhythm. She has these big gray eyes, oh, and I like all this," and he ruffles my massive hair, "and she's funny, kind, and she has the strongest thighs . . ." Ollie pauses for a second, then continues, "Oh, and I really love—"

"*Shut up!*" hisses Pearl. "We're going," she announces to The Pink Ladies, and she turns and disappears into the crowd. Only they don't all follow her—Kat stays where she is.

She looks tired. "I'm so sorry, Bea," she says. "I've been the worst friend in the world, haven't I?" I shrug. Right now, with Ollie standing next to me and my heart still thudding from our dance, it's hard to think about how all this began. She sighs and says, "I reallyass, missass beingass your friendass, Bea-ass. Can I ring you later?"

"OKass," I say. We have a lot to talk about.

Just then the No Angels boys walk past. "Got to go," says Kat, wriggling through the crowd, trying to catch up with them.

I turn back to Ollie. "What do you love?" I ask.

"Your socksarse," he says, slipping his hand into mine.

17. ♡

What do you do the day after nearly winning a TV dance show and being kissed for the first time in your life?

Make a Lego swimming pool with your three-year-old sister, of course . . . oh, and your boyfriend.

My *boyfriend*. That sounds good. My boyfriend, *Ollie*. That sounds even better. This is definitely our best Lego creation ever, because Ollie makes a waterslide that you can actually run water down.

After Lego, we wander over to the hospital to see Nan. We have to stop to pose for photos five times, but the whole "celebrity thing" is fun, especially when a radiologist asks us to do a moonflip in the staff cafeteria.

Nan tells us we danced "just like Fred and Ginger"—I'll have to Google them later—and gives us ten pounds and tells us to go and enjoy ourselves.

"Oh, Bea," she says as we're leaving, "I have some exciting news: I'm allowed out next week! Only, your mum doesn't think I should go home yet so it looks like we're going to be sharing a room again . . . you'd better dig out that airbed."

"I never took it down," I say. I go back to the bed while Ollie waits by the door. She holds my hand. "I'm really sorry I didn't win, Nan."

"But you *did* win, Bea." She pushes me back towards Ollie. "I said you would."

Ollie and I wander through the park by the hospital. In our town, it's hard to find anything to do on a Sunday, even with ten pounds, but in the end, we buy paninis and banana milk in the café and have a picnic by the duck pond. The ducks get our crusts.

We lie back in the sun and I put my head on Ollie's chest.

"Hey, Bea," he says. "I think this might be better than starring in a West End musical."

"Today," I say in my showbiz voice, "Ollie Matthews will be feeding ducks in the park with Bea Hogg!"

"Exactly," he says.

What do you do *two days* after nearly winning a TV dance show?

Go to school, of course. I give Emma a massive French kiss, then walk down the path, daisy hair grip stuck in my curls.

"Bye, gruffy-face!" she yells.

"Bye, gruffy-face botty-bird!" I shout back. She loves that one, and runs back in to tell Mum.

The juniors are by the convenience store and I go and sit on the wall, but not right at the very end. In fact, I sit quite near to them. When the bus pulls up, they've quizzed me about how much we got paid (nothing) and if Shad is "doable in the flesh" (no, he wears high heels).

Walking down the bus, I see Kat in our usual place, and Ollie sitting across the aisle. They both have an empty seat next to them. In front of Ollie, I see Bus Kelly, all alone as usual, grinning up at me.

"Hi!" I say to them all. Then, "Move over, Kelly." She is so happy she hugs my arm. I turn around to Kat and Ollie. "Kelly's got a rabbit with only three legs," I tell them. I know an awful lot about three-legged Pepper.

"I've got a dog with one eye," says Ollie.

"I've got a cat, Pinky, and she's got everything," says Kat, "except fur. It all fell out after a fight with a fox."

"She dresses it in baby clothes," I add. This makes Kelly gasp with delight, and of course, Kat gets her phone out and starts showing her photos.

"Hey, Ollie," I say, and I have to grin.

"Hey," he says back, and our fingers meet over the bus seat. Just then, I catch sight of Pearl, sitting towards the back of the bus. She's resting her face in her hand, leaning on the seat in front of her and she's looking at me.

I'm used to that, but it's different today. Even though she's surrounded by friends, she doesn't seem part of them. Usually, she is in the middle of the action, the queen of every situation. I don't look away. Then she smiles, the smile I saw when I swung her round on my sweater all those years ago, and she wiggles four fingers at me. The smile vanishes and she turns back to her friends, telling Holly she looks like a "fat pig" in her new coat.

I wonder if I imagined it, her little Ladybird wave? Even though she's not looking, I do it back, not so that anyone would notice.

"Hey, look at this one, Ollie," says Kat, shoving her phone under his nose. "It's Bea dressed as a cat . . . can you believe she squeezed into that costume?"